"WHAT

A shot explod[ed] with plaster chips and powder, stinging his face and the backs of his hands.

There was enough room for him to take a running start toward the window. Maud pumped out slugs, deafening in the small space, filling it with gun smoke.

Shots roared. One hit the window frame. Another starred a pane of glass.

Slocum threw himself out the window. Too bad it was closed . . .

DON'T MISS THESE
ALL-ACTION WESTERN SERIES
FROM THE BERKLEY PUBLISHING GROUP

THE GUNSMITH by J. R. Roberts
Clint Adams was a legend among lawmen, outlaws, and ladies. They called him . . . the Gunsmith.

LONGARM by Tabor Evans
The popular long-running series about U.S. Deputy Marshal Long—his life, his loves, his fight for justice.

SLOCUM by Jake Logan
Today's longest-running action Western. John Slocum rides a deadly trail of hot blood and cold steel.

BUSHWHACKERS by B. J. Lanagan
An action-packed series by the creators of Longarm! The rousing adventures of the most brutal gang of cutthroats ever assembled—Quantrill's Raiders.

JAKE LOGAN

SLOCUM AND THE COMELY CORPSE

J

JOVE BOOKS, NEW YORK

SLOCUM AND THE COMELY CORPSE

A Jove Book / published by arrangement with
the author

PRINTING HISTORY
Jove edition / May 1998

SLOCUM AND THE
COMELY CORPSE

1

The screaming woke Slocum. He did not wake all at once. He came around slowly, by degrees. All was confusion, darkness.

Where am I? he thought. Thinking hurt. His head hurt, ached. He saw only blackness. *Night?*

There was screaming. A woman's? Tireless screaming, going on and on, making his head hurt worse.

The screaming grew louder, splitting his skull and jarring his bones. His aching bones . . . Blackness lightened, becoming dark brown, then brown. The clinging muck of oblivion lost its hold, and he floated upward, drifting, faster now—

He realized his eyes were closed. He tried to open them. The lids felt gummy, glued-down. Groaning, he opened them.

Through brown-gray-gold murk could be seen the outlines of a room: walls, floor, ceiling. The gloom faded, reality coming into view. At the far end of the room stood an upright oblong space, an open doorway.

In the doorway stood the screamer. He couldn't see her too well. The screams sent waves of pain through his head, blurring his vision.

Abruptly, the scene fell into focus. Shadows of unreality were mostly gone now, though the room was still gloomy. It was a small single room, with a white plaster ceiling and red wallpaper. The wallpaper had a fancy pattern, like a diamond-hatched snakeskin, enlarged and infinitely repeated. It made Slocum dizzy just to look at it. Red wallpaper, dull, faded, fraying in spots. The door frame and moldings were dark stained wood.

Opposite the door stood a bed, its head to the far wall. Slocum lay on it, on his back. He sprawled awkwardly, in a stiff, unnatural position. He was fully clothed, and had on his boots. He lay on the left side of the bed, feet to the door.

To his left, against the wall, stood a marble-topped chest of drawers. On it, a serving tray held a water pitcher and two glasses. Behind, mounted on a stand rising from the back of the chest, was an oval swivel-mirror. The glass was tilted forward, at a forty-five-degree angle. Nearby, on the countertop, stood a globe oil lamp. It was dark, unlit.

The door was about six feet away from the foot of the bed. The screamer stood hunched in the doorway, holding on to the frame with both hands. She was young, hulking. She had brown bun hair, a potato face, flat chest, wide hips and thighs. She wore a brown wool dress, sleeves rolled up past the elbows, baring brawny washerwoman's arms, and a white bib-front cleaning apron.

He knew her: *Nedda*. That was her name, Nedda Something. *Maid, house drudge . . .*

There was more, but he couldn't remember, couldn't think. Not with all that screaming.

"For God's sake stop that noise!" he said, or tried to. He couldn't talk so well, had a hard time making his mouth shape the words. What came out sounded wrong, not making sense. It didn't even sound much like English.

Saying it made his skull pound as if it would burst. He touched his hands to his head, cushioning it.

Seeing that Slocum was astir sent Nedda into fresh hysterics. She grew short of breath, her screams fading. Now they were more gasps than shrieks.

Behind her, the passage began to fill with noise, then people. Newcomers, brought at last by the screams. Up rushed a couple. The woman was young, in her late teens. Her dark hair was cut in bangs across her forehead, the sides sweeping down in glossy wings, pageboy-style. High, arched brows, thin, whiplike. Wide dark eyes, with dark circles under them. A red, sullen mouth, downturned at the corners.

She wore black lingerie, sleek and low-cut, with black lace. It outlined her shapely breasts; high, firm, and pointed. Over it was a thrown-on robe, pink, with white fur collar and cuffs. It was open down the front, unbelted.

Pauline. Easy to find a name for that one. Easy to guess the rest too. *A whore, a good-looking whore*.

At her heels was an older man, fully dressed except for his tie. He had wavy gray hair and a stiff-bristled silver-gray mustache and goatee. His head was tilted back with his eyebrows raised, and he was looking down his nose, leading with it, as if sniffing the air.

No name for him. But he looked prosperous, a financier or bank officer. From where he stood, he couldn't see into the room. He was behind Pauline, who was behind Nedda, frozen in the doorway.

At first, Pauline didn't see into the room either. She grabbed Nedda by the shoulders, shaking her. She was much shorter and smaller than Nedda, but handled her easily, as if the other were made of straw. She gave her a good rattling, shouting at her to shut up.

Nedda, breathless, fell silent. She kept her face turned toward Slocum, staring. Eyes like black olives bulged in a leaden face. She unpeeled a hand from where it was gripping the doorjamb, lifting it to point a shaky accusatory forefinger.

Pauline kept shaking Nedda, slamming her against the door frame. She said, "What are you on about, you stupid cow—?!"

Nedda kept looking into the room. Pauline paused, frowning, biting her lower lip. She turned her head, her gaze following the direction of Nedda's pointing finger, to Slocum.

Pauline went white around the eyes, color draining from her skin. Her eyes widened, lips parted. Her lips looked even redder against her now-bloodless face. It was stiff, stark. She looked ten years older.

She raised a hand to her mouth, taking a step back. The gray-haired man was moving forward, for a better look. He bumped his nose on the back of Pauline's head, a painful blow bringing tears to his eyes.

"Ow!" he said, clapping his fingers to his nose.

The passage outside the door was further crowded by the arrival of a second couple, a bosomy blue-eyed redhead and a shaggy-haired, bearded man in a suit of long red underwear. Buckled over the long underwear was a well-worn leather gun belt with side arm.

He was bleary-eyed, puzzled, more than half drunk. He stood on tiptoes, trying to see over the backs of the gray-haired man, Pauline, and Nedda, into the room.

"Whass' goin' on?" he said, peering, squinting. He got a good look and gasped, stammering, *"M-m-m-muh-murder!"*

Inside the doorway floated white oval faces with gaping eyes and mouths. *Murder.*

The redhead pushed forward, thrilled, demanding, "Who's killed, Cal?"

Cal was the stutterer. He stopped trying to talk, swallowed hard, and started over. This time he managed to croak out the word "Murder!" again.

"Who, Cal, who?"

Slocum glanced sideways, at the other side of the bed, not surprised by what he found. He was not the bed's sole occupant. He shared it with a corpse. A female corpse.

She lay on her back, head propped up by a pillow and the headboard. Her arms lay at her sides. She was a brunette, young. She must have been pretty when she was alive. She hadn't died peacefully, judging by the expression on her face, a mingling of shock, rage, and horror.

She wore a wine-red dress, black stockings, ankle boots. The front of the dress was ripped open, an act that had been done with such violence that it left her half nude, from waist to throat. Buried between her breasts was a hunting knife. It was hilt-deep. A long, slim, slightly curved knife, it had deer-horn grips and a rounded pommel. Slocum had never seen it before.

The girl was more familiar. . . . He remembered her from before. *When? Last night? How much time had passed between then and now?*

She'd been beautiful and desirable and alive. Her name was— He drew a blank. She'd told him her name, but he couldn't remember it. Maybe he'd been drunk. Maybe they both had.

But not so drunk that he wouldn't remember killing her, with a knife that wasn't his.

And what was putting a hurt on him was no hangover. He'd had enough of them to know that that wasn't what was flattening him. He felt hammered.

Of course, the girl felt worse. Or had. Now she was beyond pain. Beyond, period. She looked like she'd been dead for some hours. Her skin was the color of wet sand. Her neck was bruised. A thin red line circled the soft parts of her throat. It was not a cut, it was a welt.

Her arms lay at her sides. The posture was stiff, un-natural, as if the limbs had been arranged that way after death.

Her mouth lolled open, a line of blood hanging down from the corner of her lips. All in all, there wasn't much gore, just a tumbler or two of the red stuff, soaked into the pillow and bedcovers and mattress. A spread covered the bed from head to foot; Slocum and the girl lay on top of it.

She was dead and he was alive and there was a reason for both things, but whatever it was had him baffled.

He raised himself up on his elbows. The effort cost him. He was seized by a wave of weakness. The edges of the scene were outlined by a whiskey-colored aura. Slocum thought he might pass out, but didn't.

From among the figures in the crowded doorway, the redhead shoved her face forward, eyeing Slocum. She had reddish-gold hair and blue eyes. The hair color came out of a bottle, but the eyes were her own. They looked like blueberries. They sparkled while viewing the deathbed.

"It's him!" she said.

"Eh? W-w-what's that you say, Vangie? You know that f-fellow?"

"I know him, Cal. I know him. He killed Trav Bannock and now he's killed Dolly!" She was gloating.

"Look at him, the swine," the gray-haired man said. He was still feeling around his bumped nose, trying to rub out the soreness. It made his voice nasal, funny-sounding.

Vangie said, "Well, what're you going to do about it?"

"Best fetch the marshal," Cal said.

The gray-haired man cleared his throat. "A-hem! Now, don't go rushing into anything, Cal—"

"This is a job for the law, Mr. Murray."

"Certainly. Of course, of course. Marshal Hix must be told, and will be, right away. Only, this thing has got to be handled quietly, discreetly." He mopped his face with a pocket handkerchief. "There's some tricky angles here. . . ."

Vangie gave him a horse laugh, loud and long. His face reddened. She said, "It wouldn't look so good, a respectable gent like yourself associating with the likes of us."

"Nonsense," Murray said. "I was thinking of all of us. None of us wants to be involved in a scandal."

"Well, you are involved, like it or not," Vangie said, sneering. Murray started to reply, but Pauline stepped between them. She put her hand on his chest, silencing him before he could speak.

"Save your breath, Reg," she said. She turned to face Vangie, saying, "Keep that viper's tongue of yours still, unless you want it slapped out of your mouth."

Vangie's face turned redder than her hair. Her fingers formed into claws. She began, "Why, you—"

"Keep shut, gal," Cal said.

Vangie stared at him as if unsure whether he'd gone mad, or she had. "You take up for that little bitch against me?"

"I ain't taken up for nobody," Cal said. "Nobody but him, that is. Mr. Murray. He runs the bank, and the rest of you don't, so what he says goes."

"Thanks, Cal, that's mighty fine of you," Murray said.

"Besides, I don't guess Miz Maud would want the law called in without her say-so first."

"No, I don't believe she would, Cal," Murray said.

"Where is she anyhow? Seems all that racket would've fetched her along by now." Cal scratched the back of his neck.

Pauline said, "I wouldn't be so quick to have the law come in and start snooping around if I was you, Vangie."

"No? And why not, Miss Fancy Britches?"

"You might not like what they'd come up with on you."

"I've got nothing to hide. Which is more than I can say about some people around here," Vangie said, sniffing.

"No quarreling," Cal said, uneasy. "It ain't fitting. Show some respect for the dead."

Vangie said, "She wouldn't be dead if not for that dirty murdering butcher! What're you going to do about him?" *Him* being Slocum.

"If there was a real man here, he'd know what to do," she said. "He'd've done it already!"

Slocum lay there like a lump of flesh, motionless, listening.

Vangie reached for Cal's gun, saying, "Give me that, I'll do it myself!"

Cal shied away from her, clamping his hands on the gun butt, jamming the iron deep into the holster. He was morally offended, outraged.

"Hey! What're you doing? Get away from there! Reaching for a fellow's gun! You gone loco, Vangie?"

She sneered bitterly. "Loco, huh? I'll remember that, the next time you come sucking around me, Cal."

"Aw, now, honey, don't you be like that—" Cal broke off, turning his head to one side, to look down the passage.

"Here comes Miz Maud," he said, brightening, grateful for the interruption.

"She'll know what to do," Pauline said.

"Always sucking up," Vangie said out of the side of her mouth.

"That's how you made your reputation, isn't it, dear? Sucking up?"

"If you want to know, Pauline, just ask your gentleman

friend, Mr. Murray. He didn't have any complaints, did you, love?''

"Not until now," Murray said.

"He's right," a new voice said—Maud Taylor's. It was hard-edged, crisp. "Outside of the bedroom, Vangie, you should learn to keep your mouth shut."

"But, Maud, I—"

"Do like Maud tells you and *shut up,*" a man said, not Murray or Cal. A third man.

Vangie cringed, throwing up her hands to protect her face. "Chase, don't!"

Chase laughed, an ugly sound. "You didn't think I was going to hit you, did you, girl?"

"Yeah, well, it wouldn't be the first time," Vangie said, sullen.

"It's too early for hitting. I'll just have to kick you."

"Ha-ha."

"Think I won't?"

Maud said, "Shut up. You too, Vangie."

Nobody spoke. "Who's killed?" Maud said. "Somebody must be killed to raise all this racket."

Silence. Maud looked into the room. "Dolores," she said. "My God." She spoke in the same tone she might have used to say, *The commode's backed up.* Disgusted, but not particularly surprised.

"He's still in there," Vangie breathed. "The killer, the dirty coward!"

"One side," Chase said, shouldering past the others, Maud following. He was six-two, 225 pounds, handsome, muscular, long-limbed. He was barefoot, and bare above the waist. His oxblood-colored hair was slicked straight back, with a widow's peak. A thin dude-type mustache was brown with red highlights. His chin was cleft.

He was in splendid condition. Broad-shouldered, with a tapering torso and lean hips. His belly was flat, hard.

His skin was smooth and pink, glossy with good health.

He entered the room, light on his feet. Cal tugged on his arm, saying, "Better take my gun, Chase."

"I don't need it. There's his gun, hanging up on the chair."

Slocum's gun *was* impossibly far away. Slocum thought: *What am I supposed to do, make a play for it so I can be shot down reaching?*

"I don't need a gun. Just these," Chase said, knocking his big fists together. His neck swelled. Muscles slid and flexed in his shoulders and chest.

Standing behind him was Maud Taylor, a tall woman; leggy, long-necked, and high-bosomed. Brown hair was piled up on top of her head in a crownlike arrangement, adding inches of height. She had a long face, with too much jaw and a too-pointy nose and chin, but she was still a handsome woman. She had yellow-brown eyes, the color of topaz and as stony.

She rested a hand on Chase's bare shoulder. It looked like a bird's talons clutching a pink marble statue.

It was all starting to come together for Slocum. Maud Taylor was a well-known madam and whore monger. This must be her house, the House of Seven Sisters, in Bender, New Mexico. Chase was her so-called "protector," supplying muscle as needed. The dead girl was one of her girls. Out in the hall, the others were whores and their clients, along with the maid.

Vangie was right about at least one thing. Slocum *had* killed Trav Bannock. He remembered that. Or did he?

Too many unknowns! He couldn't quite think straight. His mind was slow, fumbling. Somehow he'd been hit so hard that his wits were scattered, and now he had to re-gather them, laboriously picking them up one by one.

That took time, but time had run out. Chase started forward. Maud said, "Careful . . ."

"Hell," Chase said. He padded barefoot into the space between Slocum and the wall. Beneath his paintbrush mustache, his lips were wet. A pink tongue tip flicked out between his lips, rimming them.

He leaned forward, bent over, reaching for Slocum with both hands. Every hair on that sleek oxblood scalp was in place. He must have brushed his hair before coming out to investigate, Slocum thought.

Chase hauled Slocum out of bed and threw him against the wall. Slocum crashed to the floor, in the corner.

Chase tried to stomp him. Slocum made himself into a ball, presenting a smaller target. His arms were folded over his head, protecting it. His legs were bent, knees-up.

Chase was barefoot and his tramplings fell mostly on Slocum's arms and legs. It hurt, but it didn't do any real damage. It hurt like hell. Each kick was a hammer blow, slamming Slocum's bones.

Chase was just getting warmed up. A mist of sweat showed on his face and chest. Under it, the skin had a ruddy pink glow. His spoiled cherub's mouth was flecked with saliva. His eyes shone. He was having fun.

He wrapped his hands around Slocum's neck, jerking him to his feet.

Between the marble-topped bureau and the window, standing against the wall, was an eight-foot-tall wardrobe closet made of dark wood. In front, it had two double doors, both closed.

Chase slammed Slocum's back against the wardrobe. Slocum groaned. Chase did it again, harder. The double doors broke off their hinges, collapsing inward.

The inside of the wardrobe was lined with a rack of the dead woman's clothes, red gowns and lacy black frou-frous. There was a sweet smell mixed of powders and perfumes.

The wardrobe was deep. Slocum fell back into it, the

garments cushioning him. Chase was holding on to a double fistful of Slocum's shirtfront and was pulled forward by his fall.

Chase got his hands on Slocum's throat and started squeezing. Slocum felt like the top of his head had blown off, again. He gripped Chase's thick wrists and tried to pull away the strangling hands, but they wouldn't budge.

Chase was leaning forward, off balance. He spread his legs wider, feet farther apart for a more secure stance.

Slocum kicked him between the legs. Chase's eyes bulged, his face purpling. Now he was really off balance, giving Slocum enough slack to properly place the second kick.

Chase's mouth opened wide, but no sound came out. He was breathless, sucking air.

Slocum pushed off with his back, out of the wardrobe, planting both feet solidly on the floor. Chase's hands on his neck weren't squeezing anymore. They were just holding on.

Slocum made a fist. He wouldn't waste it trying to make a dent in that hard-muscled torso. He went downstairs, punching Chase in the crotch.

Maud said, "Dirty bastard!"

"That's right, lady," Slocum muttered.

There was no more fight left in Chase. He started to fold up, knees buckling. Slocum clapped his hands on the sides of Chase's head, pulling it forward and down, where it was going anyway. At the same time, he brought his right knee up, hard.

The knee struck Chase square in the mush, splashing his face. A sharp pain struck the knee, numbing it. Chase jackknifed backward, as if he was doing a back-flip. He hit the bed's edge, jostling the corpse. He bounced off the mattress, spilling bonelessly to the floor, inert. His face was a wet red mess.

Maud raised her fists to shoulder height, nails digging into palms. She shrieked once, a wordlike outcry. Her eyes showed all white around the irises, crazy-mad.

She said, "Kill him, Cal! Shoot!"

Cal struggled in the crowded passageway, gun drawn, trying to get through. "I can't get a clear shot!"

Slocum looked down. Something white and raw-edged was stuck in his knee. Chase's tooth . . .

He took a step forward. The leg buckled, spilling him onto the bed. He fell face-forward across the mattress.

One of his hands landed on the dead girl. She was stiff, cool. He recoiled from the touch.

Cal lurched through the doorway, into the room. In his long red underwear, wearing a gun belt and boots, he was almost comical, except for the gun. There was nothing comical about his expression either. It was intent, serious, a man moving in for the kill.

Now he had a clear line of fire.

Maud said, "What are you waiting for? *Shoot!*"

The only weapon at hand was the one sticking out of the dead girl's chest. Slocum grabbed the knife by the handle, pulling it free. He gave his wrist a sharp snap, flicking the gore off the blade.

Cal fired, missed. The bullet passed over Slocum, hitting the wall above the headboard. Grabbing the knife had unnerved Cal, whose hand had jerked when he pulled the trigger.

In one motion, Slocum rolled sideways across the mattress, raised up, and threw the knife.

He didn't think, didn't pause to aim, he just did it. It was instinctual. He was good with knives and had done a lot of practicing with them. This blade was long and thin and nicely balanced.

It pinwheeled across the room, a blur. *Thunk!*

The blade pierced Cal's gun hand, entering through the

back and exiting through the palm. It was in deep, the hilt hard against the back of the hand.

The gun slipped from his nerveless fingers, hitting the floor. The hammer was cocked, but it didn't go off.

Cal held his wounded hand in front of his face, his eyes popping. He dropped to his knees, gasping, eyes closed.

The gun was a Colt .45. It lay on its side, on the floor, in plain view.

Vangie and Maud both went for it at the same time. Slocum would have gone for it too, but it was a lot closer to them than it was to him.

He might have tried for his holstered gun hanging on the chair, if he'd thought it was loaded.

Chase was a possible human shield, but Slocum knew he didn't have enough left to lift him off the floor. He didn't have much left, period.

He rolled across the mattress, this time backward, away from the others. He threw his feet on the floor, jumping out of bed.

Cal was in Vangie's way, so Maud got to the gun first. She scooped it off the floor, holding it in both hands.

A shot exploded, drilling the wall, spraying Slocum with plaster chips and powder, stinging his face and the backs of his hands.

There was enough room for him to take a running start toward the window. Maud pumped out slugs, deafening in that small space, filling it with gunsmoke.

Shots roared. One hit the window frame. Another starred a pane of glass.

Slocum threw himself out the window. Too bad it was closed, but that didn't stop him. Those shots were getting close!

2

Slocum cannonballed into the window, encouraged by the last slug, which had come close enough to lift the hairs on the back of his neck. There was an instant of resistance, a fraction of a second.

Panes and frames disintegrated, exploding outward in a burst of crystals and splinters, swept aside by Slocum's bulk.

There was coldness, and then he was in midair, falling. Earth rushed up to meet him.

He fell about ten feet down, then hit something, a projecting roof or ledge. He bounced off, scrabbling for a handhold, and found himself on a short steep-sloped surface, then pitched headfirst off it. He dropped twelve feet to the ground.

He blacked out, but only for a flicker, a few heartbeats. He came to while he was still rolling. Finally, he rolled to a stop, the wind knocked out of him.

He lay facedown in the weedy dirt gasping, unable to draw breath. That scared him more than anything so far.

Blindly, in a mad panic, he threw himself over on his back. The ground thumped him between the shoulder blades, hard. The action got everything moving again.

15

Time ceased to stand still as he drew a breath. . . .

He lay face-up, looking at the sky. It was light, but there was no color in it, not a hint of blue. The air was fresh and cool. In the corners of his eyes, on both sides of his head, he could see golden-brown weeds, fresh with dew.

A rattling sounded from somewhere above, followed almost immediately by a tuneful *clink*.

Slocum raised himself on his elbows, looking for the source of the sound. The movement sent his body throbbing. He felt like one big bruise. A groan ripped out of him.

The scene wavered, blurring, doubling. Slocum shook his head to clear it. He forced his eyes back into focus.

He lay on his back in a yard, behind the back of the building. It was a two-story white-painted wooden-frame house. Above the back door, on the second floor, where a window had been, gaped a jagged black opening. The inside of the frame was lined with glass shards, like teeth in some monstrous mouth. As Slocum watched, a piece from the upper frame came loose with a rattle, plummeting like an icy barb into the ground.

Now he could see what had happened. When he'd gone out the window, the platform roof had broken his fall. The ground was hard but the weeds were high, needing cutting. They'd helped to cushion his fall.

Maud Taylor leaned out the window, holding the gun in both hands. When she saw Slocum, she fired and missed. Two slugs thudded into the ground beside his head, so close that they made his skull ring.

Maud swore, jockeying for a better shot. She brushed against the frame, sending more glass teeth earthward.

Slocum rolled left, away from the shooter. He got his feet under him and jumped up, throwing himself still further to the left. The corner of the house drew near. The yard wasn't much wider than the rear of the house. Beyond the corner, the yard only went on for another eight feet or so, ending in a waist-high white picket fence. The fence could have used painting. On the other side of it was a hedge, a man-high thicket of dense brown bushes.

Maud threw some lead at him. The shots missed, punching past Slocum, shattering some fence slats.

He rounded the corner, out of range. The shooting stopped.

The house was a simple flat-roofed rectangle, two stories high. The long sides of the structure ran north-south. Slocum was on the east side of the house. A strip of ground lay between the wall and the picket fence. At the far end lay open space. Slocum made for it, half stumbling, half running.

At least there were no broken bones, or if there were, they weren't enough to stop him. He weaved around a few shrubs, breaking into the front yard.

Slocum glanced at the house rearing up above him. From inside came a muffled clamor, shouting. It sounded like it was coming from upstairs. If he'd heard the sounds of someone on the other side of the front door, opening it, he might have risked lurking just outside it, in a desperate attempt to wrest away a gun when the other came out. But all the noise came from the second floor. Nobody had yet come down the stairs.

So he ran. Easier to dodge a shot from a dozen yards away than at point-blank range. He angled across the lawn toward the front gate. The grass was dead and brown, but wet with dew that darkened the feet of his boots.

The top of the fence was waist-high, but even though he was in a hurry, he didn't have enough left to hurdle it. He paused at the gate to unlatch it. It was a section of the fence, double-hinged and opening outward. He went out, closing the gate behind him, pausing to re-fasten it.

While he was fumbling with the latch, the middle window on the second floor was flung open. He didn't wait to see what would happen next. He staggered into the street and away.

Street? Hardly. It was little more than an unpaved road, a dirt road, rutted. Empty, at least in the immediate vicinity.

A wind blew from the west, gusting, whipping up dirt and chaff. Slocum narrowed his eyes against it. The wind was cold, knifing through his clothes, making him shiver.

In this part of New Mexico, at this time of the year, when fall slides into winter, the days may be warm but the nights are cold. Slocum figured it was about forty-five degrees Fahrenheit. The wind came down from the mountains, making it much colder. Slocum wore a dark blue button-down long-sleeved shirt, a fleece-lined black leather vest, gray-brown jeans, and boots. The vest was warm, but it hung open, letting the sharp wind cut through the shirt.

He wasn't used to going outdoors without a hat. His bare head felt bald, cold. It hurt too.

The sky was light, but the sun had not yet come up. Morning. When he had gone upstairs with the whore last night, it had been Saturday. So, unless he'd been out longer than he thought and lost a day, this was Sunday morning. Early Sunday morning.

The house stood alone on a lot east of the town proper. Just west of it, where the property ended, the road took a slight dip, sloping downward for a stone's throw before leveling off at a graded railroad bed. The tracks ran north-south, as far as the eye could see in both directions. On the west side of the tracks stood a station. It was closed, the platform empty. About an eighth of a mile north up the line, a trestle bridge spanned a lead-colored river.

On the far side of the tracks, the dirt road sloped upward for another stone's throw, leveled off, and spilled westward into the heart of town.

The site had been settled long before the advent of a town called Bender. It sat astride one of the principal trade routes coming up out of Mexico, a transit point for the two-way traffic across the border, traffic in gold, salt, hides, guns, and livestock, both human and animal. Here the slave trade still thrived. Girls were sold into whoredom up and down the pipeline. Men were sold as slave laborers, toiling away the rest of their short miserable lives as peons on the great estates of the land barons, or as molelike burrowers in the mines.

In these parts, the trade was kept behind the scenes. Civilization had come to this part of the West, bringing increased scrutiny and a need for discretion. And Bender dealt in more than contraband nowadays. The area was well-watered by a network of rivers and streams that eventually flowed into a branch of the Rio Grande. Good ranch land. The mineral-rich hills held deposits of gold, silver, and copper. Mines dotted the land. The mines and ranches had brought the railroad. Trains needed water, and Bender had it. Before the railroad, the town had been small, sleepy, peaceful—at least on the outside. When the railroad came, Bender boomed.

Now, the town numbered a few hundred souls, with an equal number occupying the ranches, farms, pueblos, and mining camps of the outlying districts.

Bender had gotten "civilized" enough to have the town whores banished to the other side of the tracks. That way, the respectable male citizenry could sneak across to do their sporting, with less risk of being seen by their wives and sweethearts.

A handful of small structures, railroad outbuildings and sheds, were clumped just east of the tracks. Otherwise, the slope was bare to the top of the east rise. The House of Seven Sisters occupied the north corner lot. A vacant lot lay east of it, between it and the next house, which was small, mean, and dingy.

Further east along the road, on both sides, sprawled a loose assortment of drab modest houses and crude, barn-like buildings. Some of the lampposts showed red lanterns, smoky rubies in the morning dusk. Maud's house had a red light too, a red globed lamp that sat on a table in the front parlor, where it could be seen glowing through gauzy curtains. But it had been snuffed earlier, sometime during the night, and was now dark.

A hundred yards further east on the road, there were no more structures. The road continued, stretching east across a great flat, vanishing into blue-gray haze at the horizon. Beyond, it kept on going, straight through to Texas.

The east road was deserted, bare of man and beast. If there'd been a horse in view, tethered to a hitching post, he'd have made a try for it.

A flash of movement caught his eye. In the middle distance, on the south side of the road, a pair of bat-wing doors swung open, as a man stepped out of the front door of a long, low, shedlike building. He weaved unsteadily, as if drunk. His hands were in his pockets. He was bow-legged. His feet were spread wide apart, helping him keep his balance and not fall over. Clenched between his teeth was a hand-rolled cigarette, its tip a glowing orange dot. He hadn't seen Slocum yet.

A piercing shriek sounded, followed by more shrill high screams. It came from Maud's house, where Vangie had stuck her head out the second-floor center window. She kept on screeching, waving her arms, trying to attract attention.

The bowlegged man looked up at her. Her shrieks were so high-pitched that it was impossible to make out the words. However, there was no mistaking the tone of furious outrage as she sought to raise a hue and cry.

The bowlegged man stared at her, uncomprehending, but interested. Slocum eased away, westward down the slope. The man still hadn't seen him yet.

But Vangie saw Slocum, her shrieks doubling. She gestured wildly, pointing out the fugitive. The bowlegged man finally got the idea, just in time to see Slocum slip beneath the rise, out of sight. The man's jaw dropped, loosing the cigarette, which struck orange sparks as it fell down his front.

Slocum started downhill, toward town. He took it easy, trotting along loose-limbed, not going all out. He didn't know how much he had left, but whatever it was, it wasn't much, and he didn't want to use it up too soon.

The bowlegged man dashed up to the House of Seven Sisters, reeling to a stop in the road in front of it. A gun belt hung low on his hips, almost to the tops of his thighs. He clapped a hand on the butt of a holstered gun. His eyes bulged when he saw Maud Taylor standing on the porch, the front door open behind her. She was in her robe and lingerie, barefoot. An empty gun was in her hand, pointing the way Slocum had gone.

She said, "He's a woman-killer! Don't let him get away!"

The bowlegged man stood rooted to the spot, staring at her. It wasn't often that a fellow got a chance to see that much fine high-class womanflesh . . . in his case, never.

Maud had high color, her skin flushed red from scalp to chest. Her eyes glinted. The cold made her nipples stiff, so that they stood out against her silken gown.

She said, "Don't just stand there! Get him!"

He kept goggling. She threw the empty gun at him. She had a good arm, almost hitting him. When the gun went skittering across the dirt, safely missing him, he recoiled, jumping away from it.

"You crazy, lady?"

"After him, idiot!"

He hauled out his gun, a huge hogleg, and lurched off in pursuit.

Slocum was at the bottom of the hill, crossing the railroad tracks. He was already winded, sucking for breath. He walked stiff-legged across the gravel roadbed, telling himself that if he fell down, he wasn't sure that he could get back up.

Behind him, shots banged. He looked back over his shoulder, seeing Bowlegs stand swaying in the center of the road, midway down the slope, popping off shots.

Slocum was glad it wasn't Maud. She probably wouldn't have missed. Bowlegs was drunk, he wasn't even coming close—

There was a tug at the bottom of his vest, on the left side, where a fold hung free from his body. The bullet that had nicked it immediately flattened itself into a lead smear on a rock in the road a half-dozen paces ahead.

Slocum climbed the west slope. Bowlegs stopped shooting and went downhill after him, cursing.

Slocum topped the rise, entering the east edge of town. The dirt road went through the center of town, continuing onward west into the mountains. Bender was laid out on a tight grid of dirt streets. At the center of the grid, where the main roads crossed, the buildings were thickest and tallest. None were much taller than two stories at the highest, except for the courthouse. It was three stories. It fronted the north side of the town square, two streets south of the road Slocum was now on.

West, above the town roofline, a church steeple showed. Opposite, on the east side of town, both sides of the road were lined with buildings. They were mostly one-story wooden frame shops, flat-roofed and square-fronted. Feed and grain, hardware, and supply stores, and similar places. They were dark, curtained, and closed for Sunday morning. Later, after church services were over, some stores would be open for afternoon business. Some folks, ranchers and such, only came to town once a week, and it would inconvenience them to have to make a second trip some other day to pick up much-needed supplies.

In the same spirit, the saloons and gambling halls stayed closed until Sunday noon, and the sporting houses and cribs didn't open until after dark on Sunday night.

Now, the stores were all closed. Beyond the first cross street, there were mostly two-story buildings, with shops on the first floors and living quarters on the second. The shops were dark, but a few lights showed in upper-floor windows. Clustered nearby were hotels, rooming houses, and private homes.

There were men in the road, dead ahead, five of them, charging toward Slocum. Three were in the lead, two others hung back. At point was Deputy Marshal Wessel, sided by his assistant deputies, Stringfellow and Tweed.

The two stragglers were civilians who liked to hang around the marshal's office in the jailhouse. One was named Nucky, the other was unknown to Slocum.

Deputy Dick Wessel was medium-sized, compactly made, clean-shaven, with close-set eyes, a sharp-pinched nose, and a wide thin-lipped mouth. He was carrying a shotgun, and wore a side arm.

On his right was Stringfellow, tall and angular, with a long bony fish face and a drawn six-gun. On the left, Tweed, stubby-nosed, with a round red face and a drawn gun.

Wessel swung the shotgun toward Slocum. It was double-barreled. Wessel's eyes were hot and he grimaced, stretching his wide mouth even tauter. He looked dangerous, lethal.

Stringfellow and Tweed were covering Slocum too, but their guns paled beside the big-bored scattergun. The trio halted, standing a half-dozen paces away from Slocum. He stopped, holding his hands up and open, showing that he was unarmed.

Nucky and the other man had been hanging back, out of range. Now, they moved forward, though halting well behind the three lawmen.

Beyond the cross street, on the northwest corner, stood a small cafe. It was open. Smoke came out of a tubular metal stack on the roof. Some early risers stood out in front of the cafe, on the wooden sidewalk and in the road, forsaking breakfast to see what all the fuss was about.

In the doorway stood a heavyset man in a white chef's apron, beefy forearms folded across his chest, watching.

Wind blew the scent of fresh-brewed coffee in Slocum's face, making his mouth water. It dried up quick enough at the sight of Dick Wessel's shotgun.

Behind him, Slocum could hear Bowlegs struggling up the hill, panting, cursing.

Wessel knew Slocum in passing, as someone who had done some minor business the day before in the marshal's office. Recognizing him, he swung the shotgun to one side, so that it was no longer trained directly on Slocum, but could be brought to bear on him in an eye blink.

Wessel was taut-faced but expressionless. Stringfellow and Tweed looked like they wanted to shoot first and sort it out later.

"What's going on here, mister?" Wessel said, spitting out a string of taut clipped words.

"Thank God you're here, Deputy! That madman shot up Miz Maud's house, and now he wants to kill me," Slocum said, pointing downhill at Bowlegs.

Either Bowlegs didn't see the badge-wearing lawmen, or he was too drunk to care. He fired at Slocum, missed. Slocum ducked, the badgemen flinched.

The next shot hit Stringfellow, the slug drilling into him with a meaty *thump!* It tagged him in the shoulder, spraying blood droplets and gobs of flesh, knocking him down.

He lay in the street, moaning. After a pause, Nucky and the other civilian moved forward to help him.

Wessel couldn't shoot with Slocum in the line of fire. Wessel impatiently motioned for him to move aside. Slocum didn't have to be told twice. He angled off to the side, seeking cover.

Stringfellow lay sprawled in the dirt, moaning, "Help, help . . ."

"Who did that? Who fired that shot?" Wessel demanded.

Tweed stepped forward, gun raised, arm extended. He toed the edge of the rise. Below, at the midpoint of the slope, stood Bowlegs, swaying, holding a smoking gun.

"Why, it's Rumpot Pete, the crazy drunken bastard!" Tweed said.

"Damn you, Pete, you just shot one of my men," Wessel said.

"Help, help," Stringfellow said. Nucky and his friend hefted him to his feet. Stringfellow cried out in agony, "That's my bad arm, you dumb sons of bitches!"

Tweed started down the slope. "You shot a deputy, Pete."

Bowlegs/Pete pursed out his lips, thoughtful. "So what?"

"I'm gonna take you in."

Pete laughed, without humor. Wessel cautioned, "Easy, Tweed."

Tweed made a slighting gesture with his free hand, the

one not holding a gun. "Hell, Dick, he's just a damned drunk."

He kept advancing, until only a few paces lay between him and Pete. He said, "Put your gun down, Pete."

"Like hell!"

"I'm not fooling."

"Me neither. Tell you what. You put down your gun, and I'll put down mine."

"Like hell. You're fixing to get yourself killed, Pete—"

Pete shot first, taking off the top of Tweed's head. Tweed's hat flew straight up in the air. So did most of his skull above the eyebrows. The brows were lifted in surprise as the cranium dissolved into a blood-burst, a red halo.

"Holy crow," said Nucky.

Pete dove into a roadside ditch just as Wessel cut loose with a single-barreled blast. The roar was deafening, a thunderclap.

Nucky and his friend jumped, but did not let go of Stringfellow. They stood on both sides of him, holding him up.

Gun smoke hung in the air. The blast echoes faded. The smoke blew away. "That got him," Nucky said.

Wessel advanced cautiously, walking as if on eggs, peering for some sign of Pete. From somewhere at the roadside came a shot, clipping Wessel's hat brim. Wessel retreated, taking cover.

Nucky and his friend dropped Stringfellow and ran. Up the street, the cafe crowd scattered, taking off like frightened birds.

Stringfellow used his good arm and legs to crawl to the side of the road.

Slocum was long gone from the scene. He'd been moving ever since the shooting started. When he'd set the lawmen on Pete, it had been a spur-of-the-moment gambit, a desperate ploy to get him out from under the guns and possibly away in the confusion. He hadn't dared dream that Pete would cooperate to the extent of shooting at him and hitting a deputy, solid "proof" that not Slocum but he, Pete, was the menace.

That was a break, but when you have enough drunks with guns, things like that happen. Slocum figured he was overdue for a break, and when one came, he made the most of it.

Nobody noticed him as he made his way west along the road. He kept to the sides, out of the way of stray bullets. He passed the cafe. That coffee sure smelled good. . . .

He kept walking. Two townsmen huddled in a recessed doorway. One said, "Where's Marshal Hix? He should be here, this is what we're paying him for!"

"He's at his ranch, I guess," said the other.

"His ranch! What's he doing there, that's what I'd like to know!"

"Well, he doesn't live here in town."

"He *should*," the first man said. He saw Slocum passing by, and hailed him. "What's happening there, do you know?"

"Terrible brawl," Slocum said. "Awful."

The first man nodded, turning to his companion. "Has Hix been sent for?"

"Yes, a rider's gone to get him," the other said.

Slocum moved on, not slackening his pace. He walked briskly, not running. The further he got from the shooting, the more running would look like running away. He didn't want to raise any alarms in this part of town.

Behind him, guns popped. It sounded like Wessel and Pete were going at it pretty good. The Sunday morning gunfire had roused a fair amount of citizens. There was a

Saturday night feeling in the air. Shootings were a Saturday night thing. And all the other days and nights too, but Saturday night was the prime killing time.

A Sunday morning kill was something different . . . unusual. More scandalous, somehow. Titillating. You could see it in the eyes and faces of the growing crowd of onlookers, men, women, and children. It wasn't so much bloodlust as it was a kind of carnival spirit.

Wait'll they find out about the murdered whore, Slocum thought. *Then it'll really be a carnival. Carnival, hell, a circus!*

No hat. Worse, no gun. What he wouldn't give to have the comfortable weight of a loaded gun hanging from his hip! The only thing he wanted more than a gun was a horse. Then he could put some distance between himself and Bender.

Between himself and a rope.

He had a horse, a good one. It was at the livery stable, a few blocks north of the center of town. The stable keeper and his grown son were both hard men, and the sound of shots would have put them on guard. With a gun, it would have been chancy, but without, he wasn't going to go up against them. Besides, he had other plans. . . .

On a hill above the west side of the town square stood a barnlike white church with a peaked roof and skinny steeple. It wasn't much of a hill. A dirt road connected it to the square.

The church stood alone on the hilltop, fronting east. Fifty yards north of it, a dirt road ran east-west, a continuation of the same road that went through the center of town. A path connected the church with the road.

From the west came a horse-drawn carriage, a jaunty two-wheeled vehicle, drawn by a single horse. In the seat, handling the traces, sat a lone driver. The cart came down the hill, made a turn to its right, followed the path, and came to a halt in front of the church.

The two-wheeled carriage was sleek, shiny, and new. Its side panels glistened like lacquered black satin. The driver threw the hand brake and dismounted.

He wore a dark hat, with a rounded crown and stiff brim. Under it was white hair, pink skin, mild blue eyes. A high turned-around collar identified him as an ecclesiastical person of some kind.

There was dust on the underside of the carriage. The cleric frowned, pulling from his pocket a handkerchief as big as a hand towel. He used it to wipe away the dust, his frown lessening as the dust dwindled. The sight of mud on the wheel spokes threw him into near-despair. He froze, undecided as to whether to tackle it or not. He resisted the temptation, pocketing the cloth.

The hill overlooked the town. In the distance, gunfire popped like firecrackers. The cleric took notice of it, for the first time. He squinted at the scene below, pale blue eyes watering.

"Hmmm, seems to be some kind of a commotion," he said. From an inside breast pocket, he pulled out a pair of eyeglasses, wire-framed, with round lenses. Behind their thin lenses, his eyes looked pop-eyed.

Now he could see better. "Fighting! And on the Lord's day," he said, tsk-tsking.

"Morning, Preacher," a voice said.

The preacher started, looking around for the source of the voice. It came from behind him. The speaker was a man, a stranger.

"Where'd you come from?" the preacher said. "Er, that is, I didn't know anybody else was up here. Your coming up unexpectedly on me like that gave me a bit of a turn!"

"Sorry if I startled you," Slocum said. "I saw some kids throwing rocks at the church."

"What! When?"

"Right now, when you were coming up. I chased them, but they got away from me."

"Scoundrels! What they need is a good sound thrashing!"

"Sure. Looks like they broke a couple of windows, Preacher."

The preacher sputtered. "Imps of Satan!"

Slocum gestured over his shoulder with his thumb, indicating the far side of the church. "Back there."

Snorting, the preacher set off to inspect the damage. "Looks pretty bad," Slocum called out after him. The preacher scuttled around a corner, out of sight.

Slocum patted the horse on the side, speaking softly to it, letting it catch his scent. He stepped up into the cart, pausing to take in the scene in the town below.

Wessel had reinforcements, but so did Pete. Some of Pete's cronies had come wandering out of the dive, drawn by gunfire, only to discover one of their own pinned down by townsmen's guns. They neither knew nor cared if those guns claimed to be on the side of the law. They were plenty drunk too. They hauled out their own guns and started banging. They stood on the east edge of the town, popping away at Wessel and his sidemen on the west. It was too far for any kind of accuracy with a handgun, but after what had happened to Tweed, with him getting the top of his head torn off, nobody on the deputy's side was in too much of a hurry to stick their necks out.

Pete's pals made more noise than damage. They gave him some covering fire, though, preventing the deputy's crowd from rushing him. Pete was another story. From his ditch, he was deadly. One of Wessel's men tried to get around behind him, but Pete saw the man and shot him. The man fell down, hidden by weeds, and was not heard from again.

Wessel got hold of a rifle. A shot cracked, dropping one of Pete's pals. That sobered up the others some. They took cover and began shooting in earnest.

Slocum nodded approvingly. It was shaping up to be a nice little gun battle. Too bad he couldn't stick around to see how it came out, but he had to make a getaway.

He sat in the driver's place, took up the traces, and released the hand brake. "Get along, horse."

The horse stepped lively, setting out on the path, drawing along the cart. The preacher came into view, returning. He said, "There were no broken windows—hey! What do you think you're doing?"

He scurried after the cart. There were horses in town, but there were men with guns too. The preacher had no gun. He'd have a brisk walk into town, buying Slocum some more precious time before the alarm was raised and the posses formed.

Looking back over his shoulder, Slocum called, "The Lord helps those who help themselves, Preacher! That's why I'm helping myself to your horse cart!"

The horse picked up the pace, leaving the preacher behind. The preacher's hat fell off and he shook a fist at his departing property. He shouted something.

Slocum couldn't quite make out what it was, but it sure didn't sound like "Bless you!"

3

Slocum drove the stolen rig west over the first ridge, putting it between him and the town. He soon found a covert, a small clearing in the middle of some hillocks, hidden from view of any casual passersby along the road.

He gave himself a quick going-over, patting his front and sides, feeling his pockets. All his possessions seemed intact. He still had his poke, a small rawhide pouch with a drawstring at the top. It was where he kept it, in an inside pocket of his vest. It had a satisfying weight when he set it on his palm.

In it was his money, a little over two hundred dollars worth of gold coins and folded greenbacks. He didn't have time to count it, but it seemed all there.

That was a help. Money was always a help. He went through his shirt pockets, pants pockets. They yielded the usual odds and ends: a waterproof box of matches, a folding knife, a few keepsakes, some loose change. . . .

He reached into the top of his right boot. On the inside of the boot was a flat sheathed throwing knife. He eased it out of the sheath, bringing it into light.

It was twelve inches long and a quarter of an inch thick. A Mexican throwing knife, simple, straight, a length of triangle-pointed flat black metal.

Good thing Dolores's killer had missed that. It really would've cinched the case against Slocum. Even so, the noose was still plenty tight.

Usually, the knife would have been a last resort, his ace in the hole. Now, it was his first resort. The steel felt good in his hand. He stuck the knife into his belt, pinning it at his side, in easy reach.

With the pocketknife he cut the horse loose from the traces, trimming the reins to manageable length. In a space behind the back of the cart's seat, he found a folded blanket which the owner had probably used as a kind of lap rug while traveling on cold nights.

Slocum tossed the blanket across the horse's back. That was how Southwestern Indians rode, not with a saddle under them but a blanket, in the style mistakenly described as "bareback" riding. He could've ridden with nothing between him and the horse, if he had to, but this way was a whole hell of a lot easier on both man and mount.

He took hold of the horse's mane with both hands and vaulted up on to its back. The horse was unused to being ridden and was balky, but it would take more than that to stop Slocum. He wasn't going to walk!

He showed the animal that he couldn't be thrown, not that it was trying too hard. It was skittish, more than anything else. He gentled it down with soft words and pats. He burned to be off and away, but some things just couldn't be rushed. The time spent now in gaining the horse's confidence would pay off later, on the trail. Providing a posse didn't happen along and shoot him before he made his getaway.

When he sensed that he and the horse had reached an understanding, he headed it out of the covert. The road was empty in both directions.

He rode west, into the foothills. He left the road as soon

as he could, sticking to the back trails, then the game trails, weaving a tricky, snaky path.

It was rough country, dry, sandy, with rocky spurs and deep ravines, no good for farming or ranching. Good for hunting, maybe, and, deeper into the hills, mining. But he didn't plan on going that deep.

Once or twice he saw distant isolated structures, shacks and cabins and the like. He kept well clear of them. He didn't want to be seen so his whereabouts could be reported to trackers who might come later.

He took the horse across long gentle slopes of smooth black-brown slickrock, leaving no trail. If his pursuers managed to come this far, when they reached the slickrock they would find that his tracks ceased to exist.

The sun rose, burning off the dew, eating up the night chill. The sky was blue, cloudless. The air was fresh, crisp.

Slocum worked his way north, then east. He kept below the ridges, not skylining. He stayed under cover of brush and rocks, venturing into the open only when necessary, and then as briefly as possible. He'd never been in these parts before, but he'd been in similar terrain. He was a hunter and outdoorsman, with a feel for the underlying patterns of this rugged New Mexico landscape.

Periodically he'd dismount, tethering the horse in place while he bellied up to the ridgeline to scout the land below.

Around mid-morning he came to a stream, narrow and swift. He had a monstrous headache and a raging thirst. He first watered the horse, not letting it drink too much. A water-bloated horse wouldn't be much good escaping from a fast-riding posse.

Slocum knelt at the water's edge. The stream was fast and clean, with swirling side pools. There were no dead animals lying upstream to taint the water. He cupped his hands and took a few small sips. The water was cool, with a slight mineral tang.

Slocum drank deep. He hadn't realized how parched he was, until he started drinking. He had to force himself to stop, before he swelled up. Too much water was as bad for a man as a horse when they were both on the run.

He splashed some water on his face and the back of his neck. It felt good. He lay prone on the bank and plunged his head into one of the side pools, immersing it. It helped clear away some of the cobwebs.

He came up for air, gasping, dripping. He rubbed his face and head. When he touched the back of his head, he groaned.

There was a lump there, a big one, raw and throbbing. His headache had gone down to a dull steady pounding, but now it came roaring back.

He gingerly felt out the outline of the lump. It was a big one, a real goose egg. Somebody had clouted him a good one.

He had a fleeting memory of something half-seen, a shape closing in on him, then—blackness.

It was gone. Try as he might, he couldn't call it to mind. The fugitive image hung just beyond his reach, formless, not seen but sensed. When he tried to grasp it, it turned to mist.

It was important, though. He knew that. Prickly but elusive, it clung to the back of his mind.

In the center of the lump was a raw, silver-dollar-sized wound, wide but shallow. It felt worse than it was. The skull seemed unbroken.

"Lucky I got a hard head," he said softly. Anything above a whisper made his head hurt worse.

He must have been clipped when he'd gone into Dolores's room. He'd been wearing a hat when he was slugged, cushioning the blow. Where was it now, still in the room?

A red bandanna was knotted around his neck. He undid it, dipping the patterned cloth square into the water. He used it to clean the wound as best he could. When he was done, he was pale and shuddering.

He found some tree moss, and took a coin-sized piece of it and pressed it to his head wound. It was an old-time remedy against infection and he knew that it worked. Back in the War Between States, two decades ago and more, farther back than he cared to remember, he'd ridden with Quantrill. They'd been hunted by Union troops, forced to hide in the woods and swamps for weeks at a time, and there hadn't been any field hospitals, or doctors, or medicines. You had to use what was at hand, folk-medicine remedies made of bark and roots and bits of grasses and leaves. Surprisingly, some of those old cures worked. With those that didn't, the afflicted got worse and died.

That was a long time ago. He'd been little more than a kid then. Most of those he'd ridden with were dead, in the war or after. He'd lived longer than a gunman had a right to expect. He was now full-grown and in his prime, looking for that one big score that would let him retire rich. What he lacked in youthful strength and endurance, he made up for in speed and cunning. He was tougher than ever, but his days of knocking around the countryside and roughing it for the hell of it were long gone.

And now here he was, without a hat or a gun, on the run for a crime that he didn't commit.

"There ain't no justice," he said. "Reckon I'll go and make some. . . ."

He wet the bandanna, tying it over the top of his head. It would protect him against the sun's rays burning down on his bare head, and hold the moss poultice in place.

He mounted up and rode on. The brook wound downstream in a northeasterly direction. He followed it for a mile or two, until it spilled out of the broken lands, down to the flat, where it stretched east across rolling plains, grazing lands for some of the ranches north of town.

Farther south were a couple of riders, moving away from him at a tangent, unhurried. They hadn't seen him. Most likely they were cowboys tending their herd.

Slocum turned north, keeping to the cover of the rough country, parallel to the flat. A few miles onward, he came to a lonely place, a kind of neglected no-man's-land at the boundary of two far-flung ranches.

The ground was dry, cracked, and unpromising for livestock, with stony soil and thickets of thorny undergrowth. No human soul was in sight, as far as Slocum could tell.

He came out of the rocks, down on the flat. A dry wash snaked eastward. He followed it. The tops of its banks were over his head. It was like riding through a winding, mazelike trench.

It was warm at midday. The bandanna had dried, and the moss beneath it. When it had been moist, it tingled against the wound. Now, dry, it made his scalp itch. He left it in place.

The land was more open than he liked, but even there on the flat there were enough nooks and crannies to hide a rider from plain sight.

Once, he passed an adobe house. It sheltered under a hillock on the far side of a hollow. It was a single-room flat-roofed 'dobe shack. In front was a stone well, and on the sides were small square vegetable gardens, which had been harvested and picked clean.

A child was there, playing with a stick. It was too far away to tell if it was a boy or a girl. The kid saw Slocum, dropped the stick, and ran inside the shack.

After a pause, the door slammed shut from the inside.

A bolt slid home with a dull but unmistakable thud. An adult hand reached out the window, pulling the wooden shutters closed. Not closed all the way—they were left open a crack so the occupants could see outside.

Slocum passed by, watching the shack until it fell behind, dropping from sight. He'd tried to steer clear of human habitations, but the shack had just kind of sneaked up on him.

Its occupants stayed inside, not wanting to contest his passage. It was a lonely site, far from help. In such places, if a stranger comes riding, let him pass and hope he keeps on going. No sense buying trouble.

The sun slipped gradually from the zenith, stretching shadows eastward. Eventually, Slocum came to the railroad line, and crossed the tracks. He drifted south, keeping the railroad line on his right, about an eighth of a mile away.

Nearing Bender, he heard shots.

4

No possemen crossed Slocum's path on his way back to town—and no wonder! The law was too busy to go chasing after him, too busy cleaning up the rough element in Bender.

Nothing like a shootout to occupy everybody's attention, thought Slocum. He was north of Bender, east of the railroad tracks which made up the deadline separating the town proper from the collection of whorehouses, gambling halls, and saloon dives of the vice district. Every flyspeck town on the map, or off it, had such a zone. In some places it was called the Tenderloin, or Hell's Half Acre. In Bender, it was called Whoretown.

Even though it was daylight, Slocum was able to sneak up pretty close to Whoretown. He might not have risked coming so close if not for the shooting. That was better cover than nightfall.

Now, he skulked at the edge of a patch of woods about a hundred yards behind the backs of the buildings fronting the north side of the main dirt road in Whoretown. The horse was deeper into the woods, hitched to a tree in a small clearing.

Slocum was hunkered down just inside the wall of

brush, peering out through spaces in the foliage. He was two houses west of the House of Seven Sisters, whose rear and east wall he could see at an angle. There was no sign of life at Maud's house and the curtains were closed. It was the same as the other houses. They weren't the scene of the action.

The real action was at the Doghouse Saloon, which fronted south on the main road. Slocum could see it between two buildings on his side of the road.

The Doghouse regulars were mostly drifters, layabouts, tinhorns, and small-time troublemakers. Town Marshal Norbert Hix had turned a blind eye to the goings-on there, but apparently his tolerance had reached an end.

Now, the Doghouse was under siege by the minions of the law. Hix, his chief deputy Dick Wessel, and a dozen others had the saloon surrounded and under the gun.

With Tweed dead and Stringfellow wounded, there weren't many more badgemen to call on. Siding with the law were about a half-dozen townsmen, and about as many cowboys. The cowboys all were hands on the biggest ranch in the area, the Pierce ranch.

Pierce was there too, a fierce-faced, eagle-beaked husky with a full head of thick white hair and a white walrus mustache. He and his foreman, Engels, were in Hix's immediate group.

The street was deserted, except for the marshal's party, which was scattered in bunches of threes and fours around the saloon. A couple of bodies lay sprawled in the dirt. Everybody else was safely inside, watching the show from the corners of their windows.

Directly opposite the saloon, on the other side of the road, stood a cheap two-story rooming house. The front porch was raised three feet above the ground. It projected a few feet past the front corners of the building on both sides, like wings, with twin sets of wooden stairs leading down to street level.

Hix, Pierce, and Engels took cover behind the stairs on the east side of the building. They were three big men. The porch wing and stairs weren't big enough to cover all three, but a rain barrel had been rolled from the side of the house to serve as a barricade.

Hix was bearlike, with a battered cowboy hat, short iron-gray hair, no neck, and broad sloping shoulders. Pierce, the rancher, was dressed like a townman in a brown corduroy suit. Engels, his foreman, was fiftyish, with too-long lead-colored hair and a boarlike profile.

Engels sheltered behind the rain barrel, which was more than half full. The other two crouched behind the porch wing.

All three held six-guns, which they banged at the Doghouse from time to time.

The rooming house stood so that its west side was closer to the saloon's front than its east side. Behind the porch's west wing was Dick Wessel, still armed with a double-barreled shotgun.

On the roof of the rooming house, covering the street, was one of the marshal's men, a rifleman.

Across the street, on the other side of the road, under cover of the buildings flanking the Doghouse, were knots of townsmen and cowboys. Every now and then, they would pop out from behind cover to snap a few shots at the saloon, ducking back in time to avoid the return fire.

The saloon's front porch was littered with broken glass that had been knocked out of the windows by the defenders. Inside, tables had been overturned and pushed up against the bottom halves of the windows, barricades from behind which the besieged kept up the fight.

From the volume of the firepower, Slocum guessed that there were about a half-dozen guns inside.

On the front porch, a few feet short of the front door, lay a young cowboy in shabby, dirty clothes, one of the saloon bunch who had been shot down before he could get inside.

In the middle of the road, facedown in the dirt, lay a well-dressed townsman, one of Hix's crew.

It was now late afternoon, with shadows slanting. A chill wind blew from the west, a foretaste of the cold night to come.

Movement showed in the saloon's left front window. Engels leaned around the curve of the rain barrel and squeezed off some shots. Wood chips flew inside the window frame, but it didn't look like he'd hit anything.

Some shots blasted at Engels from the right front window. He ducked behind the barrel. The barrel caught a slug, but not Engels. Water fountained from the bullet hole.

More gunfire from the right front window, a fusillade pinning down Engels, Pierce, and Hix.

Wessel loosed both barrels at once into the right front window. The thunderclap boomed on the street.

Shooting from the left window. Too late. As soon as Wessel cut loose, he dropped below cover. Shots in his direction missed. He lay on his side, breaking the shotgun, reloading.

A shriek sounded from somewhere behind the right front window, in the immediate aftermath of the shotgun blast. It gurgled and then was immediately choked off.

Some of Hix's men cornering in front of the building east of the saloon leaned out and opened fire. One of them, a cowboy, stepped into the road, angling for a better shot.

A bullet from the saloon drilled him, not fatally. He dropped, shouting.

Inside the saloon, somebody cheered. The others were

encouraged to finish off the downed man. Gunfire erupted from both windows, but the wounded man lay hunched on his side on the street, below their angle of fire. Plenty of lead was slung at him, but it all passed harmlessly overhead.

A Doghouse gun, a big blue-jowled man dressed in black, leaned around the right side of the door frame, trying to draw a bead on the downed man.

The other shot first, and straight. There was a thudding splat as the bullet struck flesh. The blue-jowled man fell forward, dropping to his hands and knees.

He crouched on the floorboards, framed by the open doorway, below the bottom of the bat-wing doors. The cowboy fired, gun held a few inches above the ground.

The blue-jowled man's body jerked as he was hit. He hugged himself, then fell forward, crashing facedown.

A shooter in the left window had the angle now. He put a bullet in the street, within a foot or two of the wounded cowboy. Cursing, the cowboy swung his gun to the left, working the trigger. A shot hit the wall right of the window, and then the gun clicked empty, hammer falling on spent chambers.

A shot drilled the cowboy. He sprawled facedown, spasming, still holding his gun. He raised himself on his forearms, back bending, lifting his upper body from the dirt.

In his back was a dark spreading stain. Another shot from the same gun added a second hole. The thud of that slug was even louder than the one that had tagged the blue-jowled man.

The cowboy stretched his length in the road and ceased moving.

Pierce, cursing, emptied his gun at the left window. He'd started to rise, but when the gun was empty, he was pulled back down below cover by Engels.

The marshal's men opened up full-blast on the saloon, laying down a concentrated volley of fire. Gunfire blistered up and down the road, most of it poured into the left window.

Gun smoke filled the road, lanced by the blazing spear points of muzzle flares.

Hix's men kept pouring it on. At first there were a few return shots from the defenders, but they faded away to nothingness as the opposing volley increased.

There was a lull as the attackers ran out of bullets and had to reload.

Gunfire broke out behind the back of the saloon. A couple of the defenders had tried to escape that way. Two had gone out the back door when they were set upon by men Hix had stationed in back.

One of the fugitives, the one nearer to the saloon, ran back to it and dived inside. The other was too far away to make it. Three posse men rushed him.

He shot in their direction, missed. They shot at him, missing. He broke and ran, away from the building. A shot dropped him and he fell, rolling.

He got on his knees, and threw away his gun and raised his hands. The trio advanced toward him.

Now that he was in the open, he was in the line of fire of the rifleman on the rooming house roof.

The rifle made a flat cracking sound. The kneeling man dropped, face-forward.

The trio on the ground finished him off. They spent a little too much time standing in one place, looking at what they had done. A shot from the back of the saloon winged one of them.

All three hit the dirt.

Hix was through playing. A couple of his men went off to the side to make torches, while he and the rest kept up the pressure on the saloon.

The torches were brought up. There was a lot of them. A voice from the saloon shouted, "Hey, what you doing out there?"

Hix put a hand beside his mouth. "Throw down your guns and come out, or I'll burn you out!"

He made sure to keep under cover. In the saloon, the voice swore, saying, "Come out and be shot down like dogs!"

"Burn, then!"

"Listen, Marshal, there's women in here!"

There must have been, because a few female voices could be heard inside, protesting, being argued down by rougher male voices.

"Send 'em out!" Hix said.

More back-and-forth inside the saloon, the arguments getting heated. A woman shrilled, then shrieked in pain as her hysterical tirade was clubbed down by fists.

"Sounds like they're having trouble with their womenfolk," Engels said.

"Whores," Pierce said. "They've made their bed, now they can lie in it."

Hix said, "We're waiting!"

"The gals decided they want to stay in here, Marshal, with some real men," said the saloon voice.

"Who's that speaking?" Hix demanded.

From the saloon, silence. Hix turned, facing Pierce and the foreman. "That loudmouth sounds familiar, but I can't quite place the voice," he said. "Know who it belongs to?"

Pierce shrugged. Engels said, "Sounds like Bletchley."

"Bletchley," Hix said, nodding. "Sure, he's one of Pete's saddle pals."

"Whiskey pals," Engels said. "You know it's Bletchley because he's got that snotty tone in his voice. He's a snotty bastard."

Hix called, "Bletchley! I know it's you, Bletchley!"

No reply. Hix said, "What's the matter, Bletchley? Cat got your tongue? Or are you just too yellow? There's a rope waiting for you, Bletch—"

A shot barked from the saloon, biting the top of the marshal's hat, shooting it off his head.

"Damn! Went straight through the crown," Hix said, examining the damage. He raised his voice, bawling, "You'll hang, Bletchley!"

"Burn them out, Marshal," Pierce urged.

"You don't have to tell me twice! Ruining a perfectly good hat, the dirty—!!!"

Hix gave the signal, setting the action in motion. While the others laid down covering fire, two posse men got on the roof of the building west of the saloon, lit torches, and threw them onto the Doghouse's flat roof.

They had tossed about five or six before those inside even knew what was happening. Gun barrels were thrust out of windows in the saloon's west wall and fired up at the opposite rooftop, at the torch men.

The angle of fire was steep, and as long as the torch men didn't show themselves over the edge of the roof, they were in no danger of being hit.

Hix's men concentrated their gunfire at the north and west sides of the saloon.

The torches on the roof continued to burn, while more thumped down beside them. In places, circles of flame began to spread to the roof itself.

From the flames rose thin lines of gray smoke, bent eastward by the west wind. The wind tickled the flames nicely, stoking, spreading them.

Soon, parts of the roof were venting thick puffs of smoke.

One of the torch men got careless, leaning out over the roof while attempting to place a brand into the midst of a corner pyre. A bullet nailed him. He tumbled forward, falling headfirst into the space between the buildings. If the shot didn't kill him, the fall did.

A posse man ran up from the east side, tossing a torch at the saloon front. It hit the wall and bounched off, falling on the plank porch, where it continued to smolder.

A second flung torch landed inside, a few paces beyond the doorway.

The tossers dodged back under cover in time to avoid the lead thrown their way.

The roof was blazing nicely now, a good hot bonfire. Thickening smoke went from gray-white, to gray, to dark gray. The flames crackled.

More torches were thrown at the saloon front. Most fell on the porch, swelling the fire building there. Patches of flame writhed up the front wall.

One perfectly flung torch arched through the left front window, disappearing inside.

"That'll burn Bletchley's butt," Engels said.

A form took shape in the window frame, holding the torch, winding up to throw it back outside.

Hix fired. The shape crumpled, falling back with the torch unthrown, dropping from sight.

"Got him," Hix said.

Pierce said, "Was it Bletchley, Marshal?"

"I don't know, but whoever it was, he's got!"

Smoke massed under the Doghouse roof, lowering to the tops of the windows. The roof was almost a solid sheet of flame. Smoke poured out the windows.

Inside, chaos, motion, curses, shrieks, shots.

A man jumped out a window in the middle of the building's long east wall, into the alley. The rifleman on the rooming house roof saw him first and fired, missing.

The target ran back and forth in the alley, bouncing off the walls. The rifleman kept shooting at him and missing.

The front of the alley was filled by some posse men. They didn't miss. The man fell, dead.

An arm of flame lifted out from the side of the saloon, into the alley, forcing the posse men back.

Part of the burning roof collapsed, falling inward, forcing flames and smoke out the windows and door.

Smoke poured into the street, hazing it. Hix didn't like that so well. "Keep a sharp lookout!" he told his men. He knew the end was coming. They all did.

From inside the saloon, a voice bawled, "Don't shoot, the women are coming out! Don't shoot!"

Smoke blurred the scene, misty, eye-stinging. A knot of four female forms burst through the front doorway, their outlines vague, indistinct.

The porch was ablaze, flames swirling around them. There were four of them, sobbing, coughing, choking, shrieking. They stumbled into the street.

One of them lurched away from the others, staggering east along the road. A couple of posse men watched the skirted form with narrowed eyes.

"Something wrong about that one," said one posseman.

"Man, you ain't lying. She sure is ugly," said the other.

"Ain't got no hair."

"Must've got burned off in the fire."

"Didn't burn off that beard, though."

"What the—?! That ain't no woman, it's a man!"

"It's Bletchley! Shoot!—"

It was Bletchley, wearing a dress over his clothes, trying to escape with the women. He wouldn't have gotten more than a few steps away, if the smoke hadn't been so thick. But a gust of wind had blown it away, leaving him standing exposed in the middle of the road.

As a bona fide female, he looked mighty unconvincing.

The two posse men swung their guns toward him, but his gun was already up, leveled. They hadn't seen it because it was hidden behind the folds of his dress.

Guns blasted. One of the posse men was chopped in the middle and went down. The other winged Bletchley. Bletchley dropped his gun, but stayed on his feet. He was a mean-faced hardcase.

He paused, as if gathering himself to make a grab for the gun. The posse man who had winged him rushed forward, shooting.

"Hell," Bletchley said. He turned, ran. A bullet tagged him in the back. He lurched forward, arms windmilling. The posse man shot again. Bletchley halted, weaving.

A couple more posse men opened fire. Gingham skirt folds swirling, Bletchley flopped into the dirt.

He lay there twitching. More bullets were pumped into him, until long after he'd stopped twitching.

One of the Doghouse women who crouched huddled in the middle of the road, coughing and gasping for breath, was shot by an antsy posse man.

"Dammit, that's a real woman you shot down there!"

"Sorry, Marshal! I thought she was reaching!"

The other two women lay flat in the street, arms held out from their sides, hands open to show they were empty. They would have played dead, but they were coughing too hard.

A man crashed through the swinging bat-wing doors, through smoke and flames. He was sooty, singed, red-eyed.

He tossed his gun into the street. "Don't shoot, I give up!"

A shotgun roared, all but blowing him out of his boots. It had been triggered by Wessel.

"Leave some for the hangman, Dick," the marshal said.

5

The next one out of the burning building was a man, a human torch. He ran blindly out the front door, into the street. He was wrapped in a blanket of orange and red flames. From a distance, from where Slocum was watching, they looked festive, like fiesta decorations.

Closer, the flames made flapping sounds, like flags fluttering in the breeze. Their bearer made inhuman sounds, like a bellowing calf. The posse men were so startled by the awful spectacle that they forgot to shoot.

The burning man staggered around in the street, zigzagging. Finally, somebody took pity on him and shot him. After he fell, he continued to burn for a while.

The saloon was a pyre. More of the roof caved in, sending up showers of sparks. It didn't seem possible that anybody could be left alive inside, but a handful of survivors wormed out of the windows in the west wall, flopping into the alley.

The all-male bunch was in a sorry state. They were singed and smoke-blackened, their garments scorched. All the fight was cooked out of them. Their eyes were red and tearing, their faces snot-streaked. They wheezed and gasped for breath, for clean fresh air. They were seized with wracking coughs. They couldn't stand. They came crawling out of the alley, hopping and flopping.

The posse men could have easily finished them off, but for now, their bloodlust was sated. Some of them even helped pull the miserable survivors away from the blaze.

The Doghouse was all wood, and once the fire had taken hold, it went up fast, burning with a thick, oily smoke, like greasewood. In the heart of the flames was a black boxy shape, the outline of the walls that still remained upright.

Inside, the roof was down and the structure was gutted. The walls toppled inward, completing the destruction.

After that, the fire quickly burned itself out, leaving a pile of smoldering rubble.

Both neighboring buildings were banded with big scorch marks. Parts of the building on the east had caught fire. The owners asked Marshal Hix if it would be okay for them to put it out. After all the shooting, the locals were afraid to make a move without clearing it first, for fear that they would be mistaken for combatants and shot by trigger-happy posse men.

Hix gave the okay and the building's owner and a couple of barflies went up on the roof with axes, chopping off the burning sections and tossing them down on the still-seething remnants of the saloon.

The fire had caught only in a couple of places and they were able to nip it in the bud.

Now that the shooting was over, signs of life began appearing on the street.

Windows were opened and heads thrust outside, something that people had avoided doing up to now, for fear of catching a bullet. A few braver souls stepped outside, not venturing far from their own front doors.

Hix and his men rounded up the saloon survivors, four men and two women, herding them together in the middle of the street. The third woman, the one who'd been shot, was still alive, but while she was being carried indoors, she died.

Dick Wessel went from body to body, six-gun in hand. One of the saloon bunch stretched in the dirt was badly wounded but still breathing. Wessel shot him in the back of the head, ending it.

Everyone else on the street flinched, looking to see where the shot had come from. Wessel stood beside the newly made corpse, his gun still smoking. He smiled blandly and moved on to the next body.

"Wish I had a gun," Slocum said to himself while watching from the woods. "A town that hates this hard is a potential gold mine.

"Before I'm through, somebody's going to pay plenty for my troubles," he added.

On the street, the two captive women protested that they were innocent, and had been held in the saloon by force, against their will, as hostages.

Hix seemed to be giving the matter some consideration. Before he could decide, a couple of the male prisoners started maintaining that they too had been hostages.

The most vehement protester received a backhanded cuff from Hix that sent him sprawling.

"We'll cart 'em all off to jail and let the judge sort 'em out later," Hix said.

"Hell, let's hang them now," Pierce said.

"I've got a rope on my saddle," Engels offered helpfully.

"Never mind about that now," Hix said. He put his fists on his hips and looked around meaningfully. "Reckon I showed 'em who's boss," he said.

Every now and then something would give way in the smoldering pile of rubble, sending a plume of sparks skyward.

Hix sent to town for a wagon, a freight wagon. The tailgate was lowered so the bodies could be loaded into the hopper. Hix roped some of the gawking idlers into helping out with the grisly chore.

The wagon driver, a teamster, sat smoking a corncob pipe, puffing away, studiously avoiding even the consideration of any labor not directly connected with the driving of the wagon. The corpses stank and the pipe tobacco helped kill the smell.

There was a flare-up of temper when some of the posse men thought that the dragooned body handlers weren't handling the body of one of their fallen comrades with proper reverence.

"You carry him, then," said one of the reluctant conscripts. Before he and his fellows could walk off the job, Hix intervened.

"Never mind about that. You men get back to work," he said.

Pierce, who was empty-handed, began lecturing the spectators. "Ingrates," he said. "You people ought to be damned glad that we cleaned up that no-good Doghouse bunch."

From the sidelines, somebody said, "You didn't do it for us. You did it for yourself. It's your cattle they've been rustling, Mr. Pierce."

"Who said that?" Pierce demanded, fiercely eyeing the knot of Whoretown denizens in the street. They all looked around blank-faced, from side to side, each trying to create the impression that he or she wasn't the anonymous heckler.

Pierce glared, arms folded across his chest. "Don't have the nerve to show yourself, huh? Seems to me that maybe we stopped our cleaning up around here a mite soon!"

Deputy Wessel stepped up and began organizing the

effort. "Put the saloon dead in the wagon first."

A posseman complained, "Dammit, Dick, why should those scum get special treatment?"

Wessel froze him with a look. "Because this way, their dead will be at the bottom of the pile, not ours. Or would you rather have them lying on top of our men?"

"I get you, Deputy. You're right, of course."

It was done as Wessel had directed. The saloon dead were carried to the wagon by their arms and legs, then heaved into the hopper, like so many sacks of grain. They lay in a heap behind the back of the driver's seat, their limbs tangled.

The dead posse men got better treatment. They were laid out on their backs, legs closed, arms at their sides. They lay side by side on the wagon bed. Marshal Hix handled the lugubrious task of closing the dead men's eyes.

The bodies lay in attitudes of repose, but none of them looked like they were just sleeping. They looked dead.

The saloon bunch lay sprawled in a mass, sightless eyes staring. They really looked dead.

Somebody found an old blanket and draped it over the dead posse men. "Lord rest 'em," Hix said piously, looking heavenward.

It was late in the day, the sun low. A slight smoky haze clung to the scene, like woodland mist.

Hix closed the tailgate, securing it. The wagon driver reached for the hand brake, ready to move out. "Hold up a minute, driver," Hix said.

He and his men prepared to mount up. Somebody said, "What about the prisoners, Marshal?"

"Let 'em walk," Hix said. He called for a rope. The prisoners looked sick, but it wasn't hanging time for them, not yet. The male prisoners' hands were tied behind their backs. They were yoked together single-file, each of them strung by a noose around the neck to the same length of rope.

One of the two captive women said, "You ain't going to tie us up with those *men,* are you? It ain't decent!"

Pierce snorted. "You're a fine one to talk about decency!"

"Now, you just hold on to your horses, Mr. High-and-Mighty Pierce! I'll have you know that I'm a respectable working woman," she said, waving her finger at him. Index finger.

"Respectable! Why, no respectable woman would be found on this side of the deadline," Pierce said, sneering.

That got him plenty of dirty looks from the females on the scene.

"Viola and me are just as much injured parties as you all," the woman prisoner said, gesturing to include the other female captive, a too-thin, consumptive-looking brunette who said little and coughed much.

The speaker was a big blowsy blonde, singed around the edges. "They held us at gunpoint and wouldn't let us leave the saloon. We could've gotten shot or burned to death! And then that crazy bastard Bletchley put us under the gun and used us for a shield when he tried to make his break dressed as a woman!"

"All three of you gals that come out got your clothes on," Engels said, rubbing his chin. "So where'd Bletchley get the extra dress?"

"The girl who was wearing it didn't come out. She's in there," the blonde said, indicating the charred ruins. "That was Flo. She didn't strip fast enough when Bletchley told her to, so he shot her and took the dress off her dead body," she said.

One of the male prisoners in the string spoke up. "Don't believe her, Marshal. She was in it up to her neck, of her own free will!"

The blonde flew at him. "Lying son of a bitch!"

His hands were tied, but hers weren't. Her rush knocked him down. Since he was roped by the neck to the other three men, his fall pulled the nooses taut around their necks. They staggered, bent from the waist, heads down near the ground, to ease the choking pressure.

The blonde straddled her man, punching his head with both fists. There wasn't much he could do but roll around in the dust bawling, "Halp! Git her off of me!"

Hix grabbed a handful of her yellow-straw hair and pulled her off him, saying, "Behave yourself, Myrtle Mullins."

She could no longer hit her man, but that didn't stop her from kicking and stomping him.

"Take that back, Jeeter, you liar! Black-hearted liar!" she screeched.

"Halp, halp!"

Hix hauled her away from her victim. She had to comply, or risk losing her scalp to the heavy hand pulling her hair by its roots. Despite her show of temper, she was careful not to raise a hand to Hix, but came along without resistance.

She said, "He's lying, Marshal. Jeeter wants to get me in trouble out of pure spite!"

"Never mind about that," Hix said judiciously. "You behave yourself, Myrtle."

"Yes, sir."

A couple of posse men hauled Jeeter to his feet, none too gently. There was a purple mouse under one eye, and his lips were swollen and split. He wanted to say something to Myrtle, but the rough handling he'd gotten from his captors convinced him that it would be a good idea to keep his mouth shut. He settled for glaring.

Hix said, "Viola, Myrtle, you ride in the wagon."

Viola screeched, "W-with the *dead*?!"

"With the driver."

"Oh," Viola said.

"And I sure ain't dead, girlie," the driver said.

"You couldn't prove it by me," Pierce said, "the way you've been sitting there without lifting so much as a finger to help."

"I'm a teamster, Mr. Pierce. I hire out to drive the wagon and nothing more. And by the way, I didn't see you doing much heavy lifting."

"Somebody's got to supervise," Pierce said.

The driver bent his principles sufficiently to allow himself to reach down a hand to help Viola up on to the seat. She was thin and didn't take up much space.

The seat sagged on its springs when Myrtle parked her big butt on it.

A posse man called jokingly to the driver, "Don't let those gals get away from you, Mack!"

"That's your lookout. All I do is drive the wagon," said Mack.

Myrtle opened her mouth to say something cute, then caught a good whiff of the stinking dead and gagged. Viola coughed into a hankie. She was a lunger—tubercular—and once she started coughing, it was hard to stop. Her face grew whiter and the twin spots of color on her cheeks grew redder.

If the smell bothered Mack, he didn't show it. He pulled a pint bottle from his hip pocket, uncorked it between his teeth, and took a long pull of some varnish-colored rotgut whiskey. Then he wiped his mouth with the back of his hand.

Myrtle said, "How about a taste, Mack?"

He took another gulp, then recorked the bottle. "Nobody ever gave me a free drink—or a free anything else—over to the Doghouse," he said, pocketing the pint.

"That's because you're such a cheap bastard," Myrtle

said. It came out weaker than she'd intended, since she was trying to breathe as little as possible to keep from smelling the corpses.

"Cheap? You're riding for free, ain't you," Mack said.

The posse got ready to move out. Deputy Wessel took hold of the leading end of the rope to which the file of prisoners were strung. Marshal Hix rode alongside him, pausing. "I'll take that, Dick."

"It's no trouble, Marshal."

"I'll take it," Hix repeated, holding out a gloved hand. Wessel, shrugging, handed him the rope. Hix threw a few hitches of the line around his saddlehorn, snubbing it into place.

"It's good to let the folks hereabouts see that their marshal is doing the job they elected him to do," Hix said.

He heeled his horse in the flanks, nudging it forward. The horse advanced at a walk, going west. The rope was pulled tight, forcing the prisoners to start forward or be strangled.

Mack got the team in action. The heavily laden wagon lurched forward, creaking. The mingled smells of death, blood, and fire tended to make the horses skittish, both those of the team and the mounted men. The posse men were strung out along the road in a loose irregular grouping.

A couple of the worst-burned corpses were left behind, to be picked up later. When one of them had been picked up earlier to be loaded into the wagon, its arm had come off. Nobody wanted to mess with them after that. They were covered with blankets and left for future retrieval. But at least the main road had been cleared of corpses.

The string of prisoners had to hustle, trotting along to keep from being choked by the rope halters around their necks.

The sun was going down, made colorful by the smoke

streaking the sky. On the street, the locals, silent and stony-faced, watched the posse ride out. The last few riders in line could feel their backs tingling under those icy stares, and glanced back to keep tabs on the watchers. Nobody was doing anything threatening, or had even moved, but their flat-eyed hostility was not reassuring.

That, and the fact that the wind was blowing from the west, wafting the corpse-wagon smells in their faces, caused the riders to move up, passing the wagon.

Hix reined in, halting in front of the House of Seven Sisters. Behind him, the procession ground to a stop, wagon and riders all bunched together, milling.

Standing on the front porch were Maud, Pauline, Vangie, and two more whores, Berga and Sue. Berga was a blonde, and Sue had brown hair. In the light of day, the women looked a trifle shopworn, peaked, but that might have been from the strain of recent events.

Maud was in the center of the group, standing a few paces out in front of the others. Her back was straight, her arms were folded across her chest.

Hix said, "I'll take that dead 'un of yours into town now, Miz Maud."

"Thanks, I'll take care of it myself, Marshal."

"Plenty of room in the wagon."

"Dolly had enough men in her short life. She can take her last ride without them," Maud said. "I've sent Nedda into town to fetch a wagon from the livery stable. I'll bring in Dolly."

"Okay."

Maud stood at the edge of the porch, hands on hips. "What I want to know is when you're going to bring in her killer."

"Soon, soon," Hix said vaguely.

"When?"

"It's just a matter of time."

"Have you got any men out looking for him?"

"Well, as you can see, Miz Maud, we've been kind of busy," Hix said with heavy sarcasm.

"It wasn't any of the Doghouse bunch killed my girl," she said.

"Pete killed my deputy."

"That was an accident, Marshal."

"Was it? Pete and Tweed have had run-ins before. There wasn't no love lost between 'em."

"Pete's a drunk. He's had run-ins with just about everybody in town."

"Sure, but he *killed* Tweed."

"He was trying to stop Dolly's killer from getting away."

"Maybe. Or maybe he saw Tweed and decided it was a good time to settle scores. Either way, he left Tweed's brains blown all over Main Street, and let your killer get away.

"If it was murder, he'll hang. If it was an accident, well, any fool that's that blind drunk's got no business pulling a gun, and it might as well be murder. A judge and jury can sort that out," Hix said.

"He's a troublemaker, him and all that Doghouse crowd. They shot at the law, and that's the end of 'em," he added.

"In the meantime, the girl's killer is getting away."

"We'll get him, Miz Maud."

"Better get him before Chase does, or there won't be anything left of him."

"We'll get him," Hix repeated.

Wessel, who'd been following the byplay, leaned forward in the saddle, toward Maud. "From what I've seen, Chase seems to have got the worst of it," he said.

"Haw! His face was sure busted up bad," the marshal agreed. "He was mad fit to bust."

"He won't catch the killer," Wessel said.

"Hell, no! Manhunting's a job for professionals," Hix said.

Maud said, "When are you *professionals* going to get on the killer's trail?"

"Soon's we get this riff-raff safely jugged in the calaboose," Hix said. He touched the tip of his hat. "And a very good day to you, Miz Maud."

He rode off so suddenly that the string of prisoners were all but jerked off their feet by the sudden start. They had to hustle to keep up.

That set the rest of the group into motion, wagon and riders starting west toward town. They kicked up a lot of dust.

A couple of riders lingered, waiting behind. One of them said, "How 'bout it, Miz Maud?"

"What?" she said, unfriendly.

The posse man nodded toward the whores. "You know," he said.

She smiled. "First the killing, then the loving, huh?"

"Well, yeah."

The smile turned into a sneer. "We're closed."

"Aw, come on, Maud—"

"We're closed!" The sneer ripened. "Not that you ranch hands could pay the freight, not on those Pierce wages."

"We can pay," the rider said.

"Get Dolly's killer. Get him, and you can have your good time for free, on the house," she said.

"You mean that, Miz Maud?"

"The offer's good. Get him."

6

Shadows were long when Nedda Barnes returned from town driving the wagon. The husky dish-faced maid handled the rig like a teamster. She swung the wagon around in the road, so it was facing west when it rolled to a halt in front of Maud's house.

The sun was down but the sky was still light. Since the sun had set the temperature had dropped about ten degrees. The winds blew colder, and the temperature continued to fall.

Most of the locals were still out on the street, huddled in small groups, talking in low voices. A couple of bottles were passed around, and soon both men and women were smoking and drinking. They weren't so hushed anymore, and voices began to be raised.

Groups of the curious started drifting over from town, some riding, most walking. They were about evenly divided between males and females. Ordinarily, "respectable" females kept to their side of the deadline, not setting foot in Whoretown. But the killings and fire gave them an excuse to see what life looked like on the other side of the tracks.

Bender was a small town stuck in the middle of nowhere. There were few attractions or distractions, and one day was pretty much like the next. Today's events were as rare as a visiting circus. One of Miz Maud's high-priced whores murdered in her bed, the killer's escape, a deputy's death triggering the Doghouse massacre and fire—heady stuff.

Townsfolk mingled with Whoretown residents, the tale of the gun battle being told and retold in ever more fantastic versions. There was a carnival atmosphere.

A gang of ragtag kids poked around the edges of the burned building. They were chased away a couple of times, but kept coming back.

The freight wagon returned to pick up the burned bodies, offering the crowd fresh thrills. Mack the driver had fortified himself with more whiskey, and could barely sit up straight.

With him were those jailhouse hangers-on, Nucky and his partner, Lex. They'd made themselves scarce during the shooting, and had volunteered for this grisly task to get themselves back into the law's good graces.

It was getting dark. Lights began to show in the buildings, shining through windows to cast yellow squares and oblongs on the nighted road.

Lit lanterns were hung up outside, on pillars and doorposts. When the first red lights began to appear, the "decent" womenfolk took it as their cue to depart. If their men were in the vicinity, the ladies made damned sure that they departed with them.

The men who remained drifted toward the local whores, and vice versa.

Nucky and Lex loaded the few blanket-wrapped bodies into the wagon. The handlers wore bandannas over their mouths and noses, to kill the smell of burning. It only partially worked. Their eyes teared, not from grief or pity, but from the fumes.

Mack ignored them, resolutely unhelpful. He drank. It didn't kill the smell, but being drunk made it easier to take.

A large knot of gawkers crowded around the back of the wagon, craning for a look.

Up rode Deputy Wessel and two sidemen. The sidemen were on Pierce's payroll, but they didn't punch cattle. They looked like ranch hands, except for their well-tended guns. They were gunhands. Hix had deputized them for the duration of the current crisis.

The three sat their horses, Wessel in the middle, flanked by the newly minted deputies.

Wessel spoke to the crowd. "Everybody get back to where you belong. Whoretown's closed tonight."

There was a lot of groaning and griping, but before it could unify into a single voice, Wessel cut it off.

"Shut up," he said. The crowd knew he meant business and obeyed. His sidemen were eager for trouble to start so they could stop it, hard.

The crowd began to break apart, whores and barflies making for the cribs and dives, townsmen on the road to Bender.

At the House of Seven Sisters, the front door opened and Dolores was carried out. The body was wrapped in a blanket, swaddled from head to toe, like a mummy. There was an opening in the wrappings at the top of the girl's head, letting snaky ribbons of long black hair hang free.

Maud stood on the porch, holding the door open. She wore a high-necked, long-sleeved black dress, buttoned up to the throat. A black cloak was thrown over her shoulders. On her hands were fingerless black lace gloves. Peeking out from below the hem of her long skirt was a pair of soft black leather lace-up ankle boots, with pointed toes and three-inch heels.

The body was carried by Nedda, Vangie, Berga, and

Sue. Nedda and Vangie held the upper body, Berga and Sue the lower. Nedda probably could have handled the body all by herself, tucking it under one brawny arm. As it was, she was doing most of the heavy lifting, while the other three did as much hanging on as carrying. Pauline followed, empty-handed, blank-faced.

Maud went down the stairs, across the front path to the gate in the white picket fence. She opened it, stepping into the dirt road, behind the back of the buckboard.

The others came out, with the body. They placed it on the wagon bed, then went back inside, all but Nedda and Maud. Nedda closed the gate, while Maud motioned to Wessel, who was nearby.

Wessel's sidemen stayed in place, bored, watching the exodus of townsfolk, who might have been a cattle herd for all the interest they provoked in the gunmen.

Wessel angled his horse across the road to Maud. He glanced at the body in the wagon, his face expressionless. Maud said, "Catch that fellow yet?"

"Now, Miz Maud, you know better than that. If he was caught, I'd have told you."

"I'm just reminding you, Deputy. A dead whore is easy to forget."

"You know me better than that."

She nodded. "You're not the worst lawman I ever met." After a pause, she added, "That distinction goes to your boss."

"Well, for your information, Marshal Hix is out with a posse right now, searching for the killer," Wessel said. "It won't be easy. Slocum's no ordinary fugitive."

Maud looked startled, and even Nedda reacted at the mention of the name.

"Slocum?" Maud said. "Did you say Slocum?"

"That's right," Wessel said, a little smug.

"The gunfighter? *That* Slocum?"

"That's the one. What's the matter, Maud? You look a little shook. Didn't you know who he was?"

"He never said his name."

"He was over to the jailhouse yesterday, trying to pick up a lead on Trav Bannock's pals. He killed Bannock for the bounty. Bannock was wanted dead or alive, so there wasn't any kick about it. It was all legal and above-board . . . legal, anyhow.

"Slocum said he was tracking the rest of the gang, to collect the price on their heads. That was yesterday. Now, he's a wanted man himself, for killing one of your gals. Life sure is funny," Wessel said.

"I knew it!" Maud said, more to herself than to him. Her hands were fists at her sides. "I knew he had to be somebody, the way he handled Chase and Cal, and got away. But . . . Slocum!"

"He's supposed to be a devil with a gun," Wessel said. "Good thing he didn't have one."

"He did pretty well without one," Maud said dryly. "What's the reward on him?"

Wessel shrugged. "Bounty hasn't been set yet."

"Whatever it is, I'll double it."

"I'll pass the word." Wessel pushed the hat back on his head. "Funny thing, though. From what I've heard about the man, woman-killing just isn't Slocum's style."

"He's a killer, an outlaw," Maud said.

"He's not wanted in these parts, or anywhere else, that I know of. Maybe he was in the past, but not now. Or at least, he wasn't. He is now, of course.

"And I never heard of him killing anyone that didn't need killing. Story is, he's even helped out folks when nobody else could or would. They even say he's done a lot of good, in his own way."

"Tell it to Dolores, Deputy."

"Yeah. Like I said, life sure is funny." Wessel pulled

his hat back down in front. "Time for me to get back to work."

"Are you going back to town?" Maud said.

"Yes, once the last of these citizens has found their way home."

"Can my girls go back with you?"

"I don't see why not."

"Good. They'll be glad for the protection, with that killer Slocum still on the loose," Maud said.

"What's in town?" Wessel said.

"They think they'll be safer there." Maud's sneer showed what she thought of the idea. "With the district being closed for business—I assume that includes me, Deputy?"

"The marshal said no exceptions."

"Then if they can't make any money, I'd just as soon have them out of my hair for a night. How long's this shutdown supposed to last?"

"I don't know. Not long, a day or two at most."

"It better not last longer than that. If I'm not making any money, it's going to cut into your boss's payoff money."

"I don't know anything about that," Wessel said hastily.

"Like you don't come in for a piece of the graft," Maud said sarcastically.

"Not hardly. Not so's you'd notice." Wessel frowned, as if it were a sore point with him. Maybe it was.

He said, "Maybe it's not such a good idea, your girls coming to town, what with feelings running so high on both sides of the deadline."

"Don't worry, they'll walk soft. They know the rules," Maud said. "They'll take Dolores to the undertaker and sit up all night with the body."

"Huh! That'll be a switch, them spending the night

with a cold body rather than a warm one," the deputy cracked.

Maud gave him a dirty look, but before she could say anything, she was distracted by the others coming out of the house. Some of the whores wore shawls, to counter the evening's chill. They all had small overnight bags.

Nedda wore no shawl, seemingly immune to the cold. She needed no bags for, unlike the others, she didn't live at the house. A Bender native, she lived in town, just on the outskirts.

Nedda climbed up on the wagon and took the reins. Vangie and Pauline argued about who was going to ride on the passenger side of the driver's seat.

"Sue's the smallest. She'll sit there," Maud said, settling the argument. Vangie and Pauline sat at opposite ends of the wagon bed, as far away from each other as possible. Berga sat there too, the three of them grouped around the body of Dolores.

Most of the townsfolk were well along the road west into Bender, with the last few stragglers footing it down the slope. The sky was blue-black and star-speckled. The moon had yet to rise.

Wessel said, "Aren't you coming along, Maud?"

"I'm staying here. I'm not going to leave an empty house at the mercy of thieves and buzzards," she said.

Wessel turned in his saddle, looking back east at the rest of Whoretown. Most of the locals had retired inside to their dens, leaving only a handful of strays scattered along the roadsides. The strays were losing interest and had started to peel away.

"They're not going to make any more trouble tonight. They're whupped," Wessel said.

"Yeah, well, maybe somebody's figuring on breaking in and stealing themselves a little getaway stake. In which case, I'll have to disabuse them of that notion," Maud said.

"Aren't you afraid to spend the night by yourself in a house where a murder was committed?"

"Be your age, Deputy. I'm not afraid of ghosts, and I can protect myself from the living. I'm all grown up, or hadn't you noticed?"

She turned to the whores. "As for you bitches, stay out of trouble while you're in town. Mind your manners and be ladylike, or by God I'll tear the hide off you.

"And if you get any ideas about running off—go ahead. See how far you get in this stinking patch of desert, with a killer running around loose."

They were silent. After a pause, Nedda asked if Maud wanted her to return after she had finished her business in town.

"I won't need you again tonight," Maud said. She told the maid to come back tomorrow "at the usual time," which was before sunup.

"Bring the wagon," Maud said. "I'll need a ride into town for the funeral."

"There'll be a lot of them," Wessel said.

7

Wessel looked around for his sidemen and didn't see them. He said, "Where'd Lonnie and Sutton go?"

Neither the gunmen nor their mounts were around. From somewhere to the east came the sounds of a disturbance: angry voices, a scuffle, a cry of pain suddenly choked off.

"What the hell," Wessel said. He turned his horse, so it was pointing east. He told the women in the wagon, "Wait here, I'll be right back."

He rode east along the road, his horse stepping lively but not fast. Beyond Maud's house, he had the road all to himself. About midway to the far end of the strip, on the north side of the road, he found his men.

On his left was an alley running between two buildings. It was about eight feet wide. The ground was bare hard-packed dirt. At the opposite end was a weedy lot. In the lights at the back of the building, he could see Lonnie and Sutton on horseback.

Sour-faced, cursing under his breath, Wessel nosed his horse into the alley. One of his men was holding a drawn gun, face hidden by shadows so Wessel couldn't see who it was. Both riders turned toward him, prompting the deputy to identify himself hastily, calling out, "It's me, Wessel."

He emerged from the alley, into the yard. Both buildings were narrow unpainted single-story wooden-frame structures. The more eastward of the two had its back door open. Light from inside shone out into the yard, illuminating it.

The yellow wedge of lamplight fell across a fat, shabby, gray-whiskered man. He sat on the ground, holding a hand to the side of his head. A trickle of blood ran from his forehead down the side of his face. He looked hurt and scared.

Looming over him were the two mounted men, Lonnie and Sutton. Lonnie was the one holding the gun. Sutton's hands rested on the saddlehorn. Both horses' hooves pawed the earth near the fallen man. The horses danced, skittish.

Inside, a couple of people peeked out the back door, not wanting to show themselves. Their heads got in the way of the light, casting uneasy black bobbing shadows into the yard.

Lonnie and Sutton had to rein their horses to one side to make room for Wessel. They didn't like to give ground, but had to because Wessel kept coming. The fallen man had to scramble backward on his hands and feet to keep from going under their horses' hooves.

Wessel said, "What's the trouble here?" He eyed the man on the ground, saying, "Who's that, Caskey?"

"That's right, Mr. Wessel, it's me, Caskey!" Caskey seemed mighty glad to see the deputy.

Wessel looked at Lonnie and Sutton. "What happened?"

Lonnie said, "We saw somebody sneaking around back here and came to take a look."

"I was just dumping some slops is all, Mr. Wessel,"

Caskey said. He indicated a pail lying a few feet away. "There's the bucket, see?"

"I can smell it," Wessel said. "Who hit him, Lonnie? You?"

"He wouldn't stop when I told him to, so I laid my gun barrel 'cross the side of his head."

Caskey said, "I didn't know who they were, Mr. Wessel! They came riding in out of nowhere—I got scared!"

Wessel said, "You can put the gun away now, Lonnie."

Lonnie holstered his gun with bad grace. Wessel said, "I'll finish up here. You two go watch the street."

"I got a couple of friends shot dead today by some Whoretown scum," Lonnie said. "Anybody gets out of line, I come down on 'em hard. You got a problem with that?"

"You'll crack down when I tell you to, and not before," Wessel said.

"I take my orders from Mr. Pierce, not you, lawman."

"Yeah, and he put you under my charge. So you'll take orders from me, or you can take off. Ride out now, the both of you. I'm sure Pierce would like that."

"That's *Mr.* Pierce to you—"

"Never mind, Lonnie," Sutton said quickly, interrupting his partner. "Let it go. We got a job to do. You can sort it out later."

Lonnie didn't want to let it go. He shook his head stubbornly, opening his mouth to say something.

"Lonnie," Sutton said.

"You taking his side against me, Sutton?"

"You know better than that. But he's right about Mr. Pierce. You go against the deputy, the boss ain't gonna like it."

Lonnie chewed it over, frowning furiously. "All right," he said at last.

Sutton let out his breath. He turned his horse, riding into the alley. He looked back, to see if Lonnie was following. Lonnie gave Wessel one last hard look.

Wessel was calm, his gaze mild, the same way it had been throughout the exchange. Lonnie spat, then rode after his partner, down the alley and into the street.

"Whew!" Caskey said. "Watch out for him, Mr. Wessel! He's a bad one!"

"He thinks he is."

"He didn't have no call to hit me. He did it for the fun of it."

"Yeah, well, tempers are running high today. You okay?"

Caskey took his hand away from his head. There was a three-inch gash along his scalp, and blood on his palm. "I'm okay."

"You're bleeding pretty bad."

"It looks worse than it is." Caskey tried to stand up, then sat down hard.

Wessel called to those inside, "You in there, come out and give him a hand."

Two grumpy-looking drunkards walked through the doorway with the cook at their heels.

The uglier of the two customers sneered at Wessel. "Those hired men of yours are just lookin' for enemies," he said. "If you don't keep them under hand, they're going to have a whole town after 'em. And then it won't matter how quick they are on the draw, 'cause we'll be comin' at them from all directions."

Wessel turned away from the foul-breathed whiner and bent over Caskey. "Just shut up and help me get him inside."

The two drunks didn't budge.

"You heard what the man said—bring him inside!" the cook said from behind them.

After some moaning and groaning, the oafs shoved the lawman aside and grabbed onto Caskey. When they had dragged the heavy load back into the establishment, the cook gave Wessel a barely discernible nod and followed them inside. Shortly after, the lock slid shut and the shades were drawn.

The street was quiet, deserted. With Lonnie and Sutton on patrol, it would stay that way. The drunkard was just blowing hot air, because he was scared. No one wanted to venture out to tangle with those two. That was how Wessel saw it.

When he'd caught up to Lonnie and Sutton, he said, "I'm going to go into town, to check on a few things. I'll send some men to relieve you, as soon as I can find some."

Lonnie didn't bother to reply. Sutton rubbed his hands, blowing on them. "Make it fast," he said. "My hands are starting to stiffen up with the cold, and that's bad for business."

"Wear gloves," Wessel said.

"Can't draw as fast, wearing gloves."

"Make sure you don't duck into a saloon to keep warm."

Lonnie spoke, belligerent. "And if we do?"

"Mr. Pierce won't like it," Wessel said, putting the stress on the first word.

"I suppose you'd tell him too."

"You wouldn't want me to hold out on him, would you, Lonnie?" Wessel said in tones of injured innocence.

Sutton said, "Send a couple of those whores over to warm us up."

"No whoring tonight. Marshal's orders," Wessel said.

"You sure you ain't taking those gals in for your own private party?"

"The marshal's orders apply to me too."

"You're sure a stickler for following orders."

"That's my job," Wessel said cheerily.

Lonnie spat. Wessel said, "Gotta go. One last word of advice. Whatever you do, don't shoot any taxpayers."

Wessel turned, riding away. Lonnie spat, saying, "So much for your advice." If Wessel heard it, he didn't react. He kept right on going, not looking back.

Sutton said, "You're pushing him kind of hard, Lonnie."

"So what?"

Sutton shrugged. "So, nothing. I just want to know if you're going to make a play so I can back you up, that's all."

"I don't need you to back my plays, you or anyone else."

"I know. I'm just watching your back. We're partners, ain't we?"

"Yeah, I guess so," Lonnie said, easing. "But there ain't gonna be no play with Wessel. I push him and he don't push back. He's yellow."

"I don't know," Sutton said. "He can take care of himself pretty good."

"With drunks and drifters, sure. But when it comes to somebody who ain't afraid of that little tin badge of his, he ain't squat."

8

Slocum was waiting for Maud.

He said, "Miss me?"

He caught her just when she'd finished locking the front door. She'd sensed an intruder in the instant before he'd struck. He'd come up behind her, before she'd even begun turning away from the door. Maybe his shadow had crossed her, maybe she'd heard the scuff of his footfall, maybe she'd smelled him. Whatever, she'd known he was there. But it all happened so fast that there was nothing she could do about it.

He grabbed her from behind. His left arm circled her head, yoking it. His hand covered her mouth. His other hand grabbed her right wrist as she was reaching for something at her side, immobilizing her.

He smelled of sweat and dirt. The smell filled her nostrils, choking her. She had to breathe through her nose because her mouth was covered. His arms were like wood, with a viselike grip.

His mouth was close to her face, his warm breath tickling her ear. "I can wring your neck like a chicken and they won't hear anything outside but you'll be dead," he said in a husky, obscene whisper. "And I will, if you give me any trouble.

"You've already given *me* enough trouble for one day," he added.

Slocum spun Maud around and hustled her into the parlor. It was filled with overstuffed furniture, armchairs and divans. Drum tables were topped with globe lamps set on crocheted doilies. Purple drapes with thick heavy folds covered the windows. Nobody was going to steal a free look without paying for it. That was good. Nobody could see inside.

That was good for Slocum, not so good for Maud.

The room was shadowed like a dusky forest glade. The whores had wanted to turn the lamps up full, setting the house ablaze with light, but Maud would have none of that. Lamp oil cost money, her money. Besides, when light was too strong, it was unflattering to her face, picking out the spider-fine network of lines on her face.

So the lights were few and kept low.

There were lots of intimate nooks and corners where private conversations could flourish between gals and "gentlemen callers." The purple drapes had thick velvet cords with oversized tassels. A piano stood against a wall, between two windows.

Slocum halted in the middle of the room, still holding Maud. She stood on her toes to relieve the pressure of his arm around her neck. Not letting go of her wrist, Slocum patted her side, feeling a flat bulky hardness below her hip.

"Where's the gun, Maud? I know it's here, I can feel it," he said, feeling around the pleated folds of her skirt. At the curve of her hip, his fingers found a hidden pocket.

It was a cunning piece of dressmaking. The narrow slit-like opening was hidden beneath overlapping pleats. He reached inside, letting go of her wrist. Extra pressure on her already straining neck served as a silent warning.

"There's always a gun, all you madams have them.

That's how you get to be madams," he said.

The hidden pocket was sewn inside her dress, wide and deep enough to hold a gun and the hand that was reaching for it.

Slocum fished it out, holding it away from him so he could see it. It was a small-bore, short-barreled revolver, a fancy little silver gun with ivory handles.

A good piece, a lady's gun with man-stopping power.

"I've got the feeling that you think you're way ahead of me," he said, "but I plan to do some catching up fast."

His eyes moved from her to the bar. Unconsciously he licked his lips. He moved away from her toward it, saying, "I need a drink."

She crossed in front of him, a step ahead. "I'll get it."

He caught her by the wrist. "You're too eager."

"It's called hospitality, mister."

"Is that what it's called?"

"You're hurting my wrist."

"Sit down. And quit acting up," he said. He indicated a nearby chair. "Sit there, where I can see you."

She sat, rubbing her wrist. He went behind the bar, keeping an eye on her. Under the counter, on the right-hand side, was a built-in cabinet. There was a ten-inch space between the counter and the cabinet top.

On top of the cabinet lay a double-barreled sawed-off shotgun. It was loaded. Slocum placed it on the counter, pointed at Maud.

"Now, that's what I call hospitality," he said.

"It's needed, what with some of the thieves and cutthroats we get in here, aching to murder us all in our beds," said Maud.

"Is that you and your girls, or the customers?"

"It wasn't no man that was taken out of here with a knife in his black heart. Unfortunately," she said.

Also on top of the cabinet was a cigar box, which Slocum brought into the light. It was weighty, its contents rattling inside. He lifted the lid.

"Shotgun shells," he said. The box was full of them. He stuffed handfuls into his vest pocket.

"That's a break. Some real firepower, instead of that little popgun," he said. "Not that I can't use the popgun. Now for that drink . . ."

He slid the shotgun to the left of the counter, so Maud would have farther to go if she was stupid enough to make a grab for it. He didn't think she was that stupid, but scared people did funny things. Not that she looked all that scared.

He jiggled the cabinet handle. "Locked."

He drew back a foot to kick in the door, but before he could act, she said, "Don't break it. I have a key."

"This is a funny time to be worried about the furniture. You should be worried about your skin."

"If I live, I don't want to have a busted cabinet. Costs money to fix."

"You seem almighty sure you're gonna live, Maud."

She shrugged. "If you were going to kill me, you'd have done it already."

"I may yet, so don't get cocky."

"The keys?" she said.

"Okay."

She reached into a bodice pocket.

"Nothing better come out of that pocket but keys," he said.

She took out a key ring, holding it between thumb and forefinger. There were about ten keys, most of them room and house keys, a few of them odd-shaped. She riffled through them, selecting a small flat key. She held out the ring, the key point-up. "That's it," she said.

He took it and told her to sit. She sat.

He stood on one side of the cabinet, clear of it, and fit

the key into the lock. He leaned over on one side, still keeping clear of the cabinet. He didn't know if there was some sort of device inside, rigged to blast unwary intruders.

But the cabinet was just a cabinet, the unlocked door swinging freely open and outward, unencumbered by any tripwire that would grow taut and then pull the trigger of a hidden gun.

Inside were plenty of bottles of whiskey. There were glasses under the counter, but he didn't bother with them. He took a bottle, uncorking it with his teeth. Reddish-brown liquid sloshed, the fumes burning his eyes. His stomach rumbled.

He took a long pull. It burned, then numbed. His face reddened, eyes tearing.

Maud sneered. "Can't take it, huh?"

Slocum brushed his eyes with the edge of his sleeve. Dubiously he eyed the whiskey bottle label.

He said, " 'Bottled in bond' . . . hell! You've been switching bottles. That's not bonded whiskey, it's six-snake rotgut!"

"Like you could tell the difference," she said. "If you don't like it, don't drink it."

"Who said I don't like it?" He took another drink and shuddered. "Grows on you."

The booze sent heat through him. There was a tingling at the back of his head. He felt as if he was floating free of his fatigued body. "I better lay off for now," he said.

"Can't take it," Maud said. "Pass that bottle this way."

He shook his head. "I wouldn't trust you with a bottle in your hands."

"You've got a gun. What're you, yellow?"

"Yeah," he said.

"It's a hell of a thing when I can't even get a drink of my own whiskey!"

"Maybe later."

Maud sat back, looking pleased. At least there would be a later. That was something.

Slocum said, "Where's the blue stone?"

"The what?"

Slocum laughed. She said, "What's so funny?"

"You look like a dog that's just had a juicy bone snatched out from between its jaws," he said. "I could almost believe that you didn't know about the stone. Almost.

"But then, every whore's got to have something of an actress in her, and a whore turned madam's got to have more than most."

"I learned to lie from men."

"Don't be so modest. I'm sure you managed to figure it out all by yourself."

"I learned it from your mother," she said.

"You could do worse. But let's leave Ma out of this," he said. "Who gave Dolores the stone, Maud?"

"You tell me."

"I could," he said, "but right now, I've got bigger fish to fry. Where's the stone?"

"Don't you have it?" She tried to look and sound bored, but greed kept getting in the way.

"No, do you?"

"No."

"We'll see," he said. "Take off your clothes."

9

Maud sat up, stiff-backed. Slocum said, "You ain't stripping."

"You're damned right I'm not!"

He sighed. "I don't have time to fool with a lot of games, lady. Do it."

"Like hell!"

"You know who I am?"

"Mister, I don't know you from Adam, and I don't want to!"

"The name's Slocum. Maybe you heard of me."

She had, but she wasn't giving away anything. "Never heard of you. Why? Are you supposed to be somebody?"

"A bad man to fool with."

"Yeah, well, I never heard of you. Slocum? The name means nothing to me."

"I can believe that. Otherwise, you'd have known better than to cross me and leave me alive."

"Too bad I missed."

"Yeah, too bad. You're mixing in something that's bigger than you think, Maud. If you knew how big it was, you'd be scared. I want that blue stone."

"I haven't got it," she said simply.

"Prove it."

"I'm not taking off my clothes!"

"You will or I will. One way or another, it's gonna get done. It's not you I want, it's the stone."

"I don't have it."

"I have to be sure you're not hiding it under your clothes."

"I bet," she said sarcastically.

"Get to it. It's not like you never took your clothes off for a man before. Pretend I'm paying for it, if that'll make you any more comfortable."

"You'll pay," she said. She unbuttoned her cuffs, then her collar. She rose, garments rustling. She unbuttoned the dress down the front, to her waist. She pulled the top off her shoulders, baring them. She stood staring at him, blank-faced. She pulled her arms out of the sleeves, letting the top fall around her waist. Under it she wore a white slip, low-cut, with thin shoulder straps. Her skin was pink, rosy. The plunging V neckline bared the inner curves of her full breasts. Her nipples were outlined against the taut fabric.

She worked the dress off her hips and leaned forward from the waist, until her breasts threatened to spill out of her slip. She wiggled her hips as she pulled down the dress. It slid down her long legs, falling in folds at her booted feet.

The white linen wrapper came down to the middle of her thighs. Under it she wore black lace knickers, dark stockings, and ankle boots.

Around her neck hung a gold chain. Something dangled on the end of it, buried between her breasts.

Slocum pointed. "What's that?"

"Why, those're my tits, honey," she cooed.

"Don't be funny," he said, crossing to her. He hooked a finger under the chain, lifting it, fishing the object dangling at its end up and out of her bosom.

It was a key, a small flat key. "No sapphire," she said.

"What's the key to?"

"My diary."

"That should make some interesting reading."

"I didn't know you could read."

"I can't. I'll look at the pictures," he said. He let go of the chain, letting the key fall back against her flesh.

"Give me your dress and no tricks," he said.

She stepped out of the dress puddled around her ankles, picked it up, handed it to him. He stepped back, eyeing her. He perched a hip on the edge of the bar, leaning there while he turned out all the pockets in the dress, methodically, one by one. He felt through the folds for hidden pockets, found none. He checked the inner lining, making sure that the stone hadn't been sewn inside. It hadn't.

"Can I have my dress back now?"

Slocum set it aside, out of the way. "No. Take off your shoes."

She sat down, unlaced her ankle boots, and took them off. He examined them, checking for hollow heels, hidden compartments, finding none.

"Keep going," he said. She stood up, raising her arms over her head to pull off her wrapper. She squirmed out of it, bare from the waist up. Her flesh was creamy and glowing. Her nipples were dark pink, long, with neat round circles.

She bunched up her wrapper and threw it at him. She stood with her hands on her hips, glaring. He patted down the garment, kneading it, making sure there was no stone.

He looked at her. "Don't stop now." His mouth was a little dry.

"Bastard," she said. She took off her knickers and stepped out of them, now bare but for a pair of dark stockings that were held in place by round garters. She had round hips, a taut rounded belly, and a brown bush, thick, but neatly trimmed at the edges.

There was no place in the knickers to hide the stone. No place on her either.

"Getting a good look, you bastard?"

"Yeah."

"You want to look up my snatch?"

"That won't be necessary. It would be kind of painful to hide the stone there," he said.

"Are you satisfied now that I don't have it?"

"Not on you anyway."

She gave an exasperated snort. "Oh, for crissakes!"

He reached out and plucked the key and chain from her neck, breaking the catch.

"Hey! Give that back!" she said.

"What's that key open, I wonder."

"Give it back!"

"That's the most outrage you've shown yet—"

She tried to knee him in the groin, but he was expecting that and turned to the side so his thigh caught the blow. It hurt, numbing deep into the muscles. Her fingernails tore at his eyes. He batted them away, but it was just a feint. She darted past him, toward the shotgun on the bar.

He got a hand around her throat, stopping her. He held her at arm's length. She tore at his hand with both of hers, but couldn't break his grip. He backed her into a wall and lifted her up, one-handed, until her feet were off the floor. Her eyes bulged and her face was red, then purple-red. Her heels drummed against the wall. She made strangling noises.

He released his grip. She slid down the wall and sat down on the floor, hard, her legs sticking out in front of her. She sucked wind, great gulping gasps.

After a while, her eyes stopped bulging so much, and her face lost some of its plummy color.

"Get dressed," Slocum said.

10

The key was to a safe in the closet of Maud's second-floor bedroom. Slocum went to it straight off, with no hesitation.

"Bastard! How'd you know it was there? Who told you?" Maud demanded.

"I found it earlier, when I first broke into the house. I was looking for a weapon," he said pleasantly. He could afford to be pleasant.

Maud was fit to be tied. In fact, she *was* tied, hog-tied with a couple of sashes from her robes. She lay fully clothed on her belly on the bedroom floor, hands tied behind her back, ankles tied, and wrists and ankles tied together so that her limbs formed a sort of bow. He hadn't wanted to tie her, but when she saw that he was going for the safe, she'd made such a fuss that he'd had to restrain her. It was that or tap her out on the back of the skull with a gun barrel. He didn't want to do that—it could damage the barrel, take it out of true.

Her room was the biggest on the second floor. It was in the back of the house, away from the street. There was a big brass bed and a full-length mirror and some dressers. There were rich fabric hangings and fancy trimmings. A lamp turned low supplied dusky bronze light.

A heavy scent mixed from sweet-smelling powders, perfumes, and lotions tickled Slocum's nose. He squatted in the closet, the door open to let in the light and to allow him to keep an eye on Maud, who lay on the floor nearby.

The safe stood in the corner, a squat bulky metal cube with a pair of flanges protruding at the base, bracketing the door. In the flanges were holes, through which had been driven railroad spikes, nailing the box to a floor beam. It couldn't be easily removed. But he had the key.

The key still trailed the twin halves of the broken necklace that had held it around Maud's neck. The safe had an inset lock and a handle, no dial. The key fit, turning in the lock. Slocum levered the handle, opening the door.

Inside was a six-gun, loaded but rusty. He didn't need it. He had other, better weapons. There was a packet of letters, tied with a bow. Love letters. Nothing in it for him. There was another, larger envelope, containing legal papers and documents: deeds and titles to various pieces of property, including the house, and some railroad bonds and the like. He leafed through them, looking for—what? He wasn't sure. There was nothing there that spoke to him of murder.

There was a brick-sized wad of greenbacks, a couple hundred dollars worth. There was a small leather pouch with almost a hundred dollars in gold coins. A larger, doeskin pouch with a drawstring held jewelry.

Eyes narrowed, Slocum emptied the pouch on the naked floorboards. There were strands of pearls, bracelets, rings, pendants, pins, and other jewelry.

"Found what you're lookin' for yet?" Maud asked with a scowl.

"Not exactly, but this might just do for the time being."

"Wait a second, mister, that stuff is goin' right back

where you found it. You've no right to pocket any of it.''

''I'm thinkin' that this loaded gun I got right here gives me all the rights I need,'' Slocum said. ''And since you won't tell me what I need to know....''

Maud rolled her eyes. ''How many times do I have to tell you that I don't have the damn stone? No matter how much you threaten me or how long you put your dirty fingers through my drawers, you're not gonna find the blasted thing. So I swear, if you don't give me back my stuff, you dirty bastard...'' ''Listen up, Maud, before you go off cussing a blue streak again. I've got a proposition for you.''

She told him what he could do with himself.

''No, it's not that kind of proposition,'' he said. ''This is business, strictly business.''

He sat down on the edge of the bed. She twisted around on her belly, turning so she could see him. She stared up at him, neck taut, face red, eyes hard.

He bounced the jewel pouch on his palm, jingling it. There was something almost hypnotic in the movement, fascinating her like a fluted pipe charms a snake.

He said, ''How'd you like to earn back these trinkets?''

That broke the spell. She said, ''They're mine, dammit, and so is the money you stole!''

''Possession is nine-tenths the law. And what I've mainly got possession of is *you*, Maud ... or did you forget? The fact of it is that you're gonna do what I say anyhow, so you might as well get something out of it.''

''Or else what? You'll kill me? You're going to do it anyway, so why should I help you?''

''I'm no woman-killer,'' Slocum said, ''and you know it, or you wouldn't be arguing with me, trying to cut yourself a better deal.''

''Deal? What deal?''

''I'm getting to that. I've got guns and money now. If

I was you, I'd be listening real close to what I've got to say.''

Maud rolled her eyes yet again, but remained silent.

"That's better. Now, just think for a minute. I'm standing here with all your money and a weapon, and yet I still haven't killed you. Why would I try to bargain with you if I was the killer?''

'' 'Cause you think I know—''

"Oh, shut up and hear me out," Slocum said. "If Dolores had that stone—and I think we both know that she did—then we gotta assume that her killer has it now. I don't think somebody'd be stupid enough to murder her without havin' that gem in their possession first. So, if you don't have it and I don't have it, then the killer probably ain't in this room.''

He looked to make sure she was following him. Satisfied that she was, he went on. "Now, we both have a stake in finding the real murderer here. Obviously, I gotta clear my name. And you'd just like to see the guy caught since he got one of your girls. Not to mention the fact it'd get me out of your hair. So, I suggest a little give-and-take.''

"What exactly do you think I can do for you outside of the skills of my profession?" she asked.

"You can tell me all you know about the strangers you've had comin' in and out of this place. 'Cause it may very well be that the murderer was a customer of yours.''

He paused as another thought came to him: "Or a stranger who sneaked in.''

"Mister, nobody sneaks into this house.''

Slocum raised one eyebrow. "I did, tonight.''

11

Slocum tried on a coat that Chase had left behind. It was loose in the shoulders and tight in the waist, but it was warm. Eyeing himself in the mirror, Slocum said, "Makes me look a little like a pimp, but it'll do."

"Chase's no pimp! I'm a high-class madam and I don't need a pimp! Wouldn't have any truck with one! I run this house, and nobody else, see?"

"Don't get yourself into an uproar, Maud."

Slocum held the sawed-off shotgun in one hand, and the jewelry box in the other. He dropped the bag into a coat pocket. Maud stood nearby, untied, chafing her wrists. When the jewels vanished into his pocket, she bristled.

"Mind your manners, Maud. I'd hate to have to whomp you in the head with this here gun butt. No telling but what it might trigger a couple of shotgun blasts, and then the fat'd really be in the fire. Not to mention somebody might accidentally get their head blown off, or something."

She relaxed slightly, at least to the extent of looking as if she might not immediately fly at his face with her fingernails. Unless she saw an opening.

He picked up a lamp, holding it at the base. Gesturing toward the door with the sawed-off, he said, "After you."

She gave him a sidelong glance, calculating. "Where we going?"

"Out. Go now. Don't get too far ahead. I'd hate to have this big gun go off in a small space like this. It'd scare me half to death."

She went through the door into the hall, Slocum following. Above, the oval of light from the lamp glided across the ceiling.

"Dolores's room," Slocum said.

Maud glanced back over her shoulder at him, frowning. "What're you, a ghoul?"

"Inside," he said, indicating a closed door across the hall.

Maud went to it, stalling as she stood in front of the door. A cold draft leaked out from under the door and through the hairline-slitted gap where the door met the frame.

"Go on," Slocum said.

Maud bit her lower lip, palming the doorknob. The door opened inward on a dark room. A blast of cold air came rushing out, raising a shiver from Maud. She hugged her arms, rubbing them for warmth.

"Afraid of ghosts?" he said.

"No!"

A nudge from behind sent her across the threshold, into the room. He followed on her heels, forcing her to advance. Lamp glow burst into the space, shouldering aside the cold dark.

The view was bleak. The body was gone, of course, and so were the bloody bedclothes that had served as an impromptu shroud. The bare mattress had been flipped, turned over so its stained side was down. A blanket had been nailed over the hole where the window had been. It did a poor job of keeping out the cold. The room must have been fifteen degrees colder than the rest of the house. Maud could see her breath, a ghostly streamer of vapor. She shivered, teeth chattering.

The floor below the window was sprinkled with glittering frosted crystals, which were fragments of broken glass. They flashed and glinted in the lamplight.

Slocum turned up the wick, brightening the flame. The light filling the room was bright without warmth, clinical. On the floor near the door were dried bloodstains, probably from Cal's hand when it was nailed with the throwing knife.

The blanket over the window couldn't keep out the cold just as it couldn't keep out Slocum. Earlier, after dark, he'd bellied up to the back of the house, shimmied up the post to the porch roof, and clambered through the window frame into the dead girl's room. The house had been deserted, its occupants outside, preparing for the wagon ride. He'd crept downstairs and watched them depart, all but Maud and the two guns left behind on patrol by Wessel. . . .

Now, Maud said, "It *is* true that a murderer returns to the scene of the crime. I always thought that was something that only happened in books."

"Sorry to disappoint you, but I'm no murderer," Slocum said. "If you want to see something interesting, take a look at the mirror on top of that bureau there."

From where they stood facing the bed, the bureau stood with its back against the wall on the right-hand side. The mirror was swivel-mounted between two upright posts. It was tilted at a forty-five-degree angle toward the bed. On the bureau top before it sat a now-dark lamp.

Maud, bored and anxious, said, "I see it. So what?"

Slocum crossed to the bureau, turning so he half faced her. She avoided glancing at the door.

"You'd never make it, Maud."

She shrugged. "I hear you, big man."

He set aside the dark lamp, putting the lit globe in its place. Light reflected from the mirror behind it, streaming on the bed.

"The killer did that," Slocum said. "He—or she—needed light to make sure the scene was rigged just so."

"You sure know a lot about it."

"I noticed the mirror and lamp in the morning, but I didn't put it together until later. That lets me off the hook."

Maud's laughter was a caw. "How do you figure?" she jeered.

"A man who rigged the mirror for more light wouldn't have stayed all night to get caught with the body in the morning."

"That proves nothing. Drunks do funny things. They can be fussy as old maids sometimes, right until they pass out. And you sure were drunk last night."

"I wasn't drunk."

"You had a skinful," she said. "And then there's crazy people. What they do doesn't have to make sense. They're crazy."

"So, I'm either a drunk or crazy, eh?"

"Mister, you said it, not me."

"I'd hate to have you on a jury deciding my fate," he said thoughtfully.

"I'd like to put the noose around your neck myself."

"Careful you don't hang yourself in the process."

She shrugged. "Seen enough?"

"Let's go."

Below, there was a pounding on the front door.

Slocum mouthed the word "Who?"

She shook her head.

More pounding, louder.

Maud breathed, "What'll I do?"

"See who it is," Slocum said.

12

"We're closed," Maud said.

She stood pressed up against the inside of the locked front door. It was dim in the hall, the only light coming from a lamp beyond the archway, at the head of the parlor. Indirect light, mustard-colored. Dark mustard.

On the other side of the door, outside, were Lonnie and Sutton. Lonnie's boot heels clattered like hooves on the porch. He was noisy. He kept thumping against the door. He was drunk. Sutton stood on the stairs, holding the rail, one foot on the top step. He kept shushing Lonnie and calling him to come away.

Lonnie was having none of it. He hammered the door with his fist. Maud said through the door, "No gentlemen callers tonight! Go away!"

"We ain't no gentlemen!" Lonnie bellowed.

"We're closed, by order of the marshal!"

"We're working for him! Open up in the name of the law!"

"Pssst! Lonnie, hush up," Sutton said.

"No!"

Maud said, "Go away!"

"Hell, no!"

"Dammit, Lonnie, they'll hear your bawling clear into town," Sutton said.

"What the hell you mean bawling, Sutton." Lonnie's voice turned meaner, becoming more focused. "Damn you anyways!"

"Easy, Lonnie . . ."

"Don't crowd me, you son of a bitch."

"Take it easy."

"Don't crowd me."

"I'm not crowding you, partner."

"I ain't funning."

"I know you're not."

"My bottle's empty." After a pause, there was a gunshot, simultaneous with the sound of breaking glass as a bullet whizzed right past Maud's head.

Maud started, stifling a gasp. Outside, Lonnie crowed, "Haw! I could pick a bottle right out of the air! Some shooting, whew!"

Maud was aware of a dark rushing mass silently closing in on her—Slocum. He brushed her aside, a casual-seeming gesture with his forearm that sent her hurtling off balance sideways.

He pulled open the door, sending it crashing backward on its hinges. The doorway framed Lonnie, standing a few paces away on the porch. He was turned facing the street, a smoking pistol in his hand. He was unsteady on his feet, swaying. Beyond and to the right of him, standing on the stairs, was Sutton.

Lonnie had time to glance over his shoulder at the open door, but no time to do anything more than that, because that was when Slocum cut loose with a single-barreled blast from the sawed-off shotgun and Lonnie ran out of time.

The blast chopped Lonnie in the middle, throwing him

down, dead. The red-and-yellow muzzle flare underlit Slocum, making him look fiendish.

Sutton was paralyzed. As the shotgun bore swung toward him, he opened his mouth to scream.

The blast roared. Sutton was still clutching the railing for the stairs. He death-spasmed, tearing the rail loose from where it was fastened at the top of the stairs. He lay in a heap at the bottom of the stairs.

Slocum ducked back inside, behind the cover of the door frame. Wind sucked out long serpents of gunsmoke from the twin bores, sailing them into the night.

Slocum broke the shotgun, shucking out the spent cartridges. They hit the floor, rolling in little half circles. He fed in two fresh rounds and closed the piece.

He peeked outside. The scene was unchanged. Distant echoes of the blasts rolled outward, fading in the night's unseen horizons.

13

Maud still lay sprawled on the floor, where she'd fallen when he swept her aside to deal with the intruders.

He went to her, causing her to cry out when she saw him bearing down on her. He was huge, a big bat-shaped form looming out of the shadows, grim-faced. But he was light-footed, his footfalls no more than whispers . . . the breaths of whispers.

He caught her by the arm and lifted her to her feet in one motion. He swung her around, propelling her across the hall, her feet barely touching the floor.

In the parlor, across the back of a chair, lay the cloak which she had worn earlier, when she went outside to the wagon. He draped it over an arm, the one which was steering her. Her arm was numb where he gripped it.

He held her under the archway, pausing to blow out the lamp on the drum table. Firelight glittered in his eyes, and his taut face was golden, with inky shadows. There was a *whump!* as the flame was snuffed out.

Maud was rushed to the open doorway and through it, onto the porch. The cold night air threw into contrast the reek of gun smoke that hung heavy in the hall. There was something nasty about it, almost fecal . . . or perhaps that stench came from the bodies.

It wasn't until she was outside that she dug in her heels, stiffening. Horrified, she said, "Why'd you kill them? I could've gotten rid of them without bloodshed!"

"Once that noisy bastard fired his gun, there was nothing else to do. Somebody's sure to come to investigate, so what's a few more gunshots?"

"You could've taken them alive!"

"I've already got a hostage," he said, tugging at her wrist. He crossed the porch, pulling her after. Lonnie lay hanging half on the porch and half on the stairs. He lay head-down, face-up. Moonlight shone on his face. His eyes were open. Wide open, bulging.

Blood glistened on porch and stairs. Maud tried as best she could to avoid stepping in it, without success.

Lonnie's middle was a wreck, but except for some splattered gore, his face was surprisingly undamaged, intact. Not so with Sutton. The blast had caught him high, in the head and shoulders. Most of his face was in shadow, but even the part she glimpsed was more than enough for Maud. She didn't look that way again.

Sutton's gun was still in the holster. It was clean, unfouled. Slocum stuck it in the top of his pants, at the hip, butt-out.

He walked Maud up the path and through the gate into the street. Farther east along the north side of the road, tied to a hitching post, were the dead men's horses. They were the only life in view, apart from Slocum and Maud. The street was empty, and in the windows of the houses, not so much as the corner of a curtain could be seen being lifted. Nobody stuck their heads outside to see what the latest gunplay was all about.

West, across the cut, in town, there were lights, motion.

"They'll be coming soon, but we won't be here," Slocum said, dragging Maud toward the horses.

The animals were spooked, edgy. Their eyes rolled and

they sidled away as the humans approached. One reared up, breaking its tether. It whirled, running away. It plunged east, galloping along the road.

Slocum swore. The other horse shied away, its taut reins stretched to the breaking point. Slocum had to let go of Maud to get a hand free. She fell.

Slocum grabbed hold of the horse's head harness. He pulled its head down, so it couldn't rear. He unhitched the reins, swinging up into the saddle.

Once he got the horse under him, there was no way it was getting away from him. With a skittish horse, reins, and a sawed-off shotgun, he had his hands full. He made ready to butt-stroke the animal between the ears to gentle it, but once it felt the touch of a sure rider in the saddle, it stopped fighting him.

Maud had stood up with a huff and started brushing off her skirts. "You know, I'm likin' this so-called deal we got goin' here less and less. I may be a whore, but you could treat me like a human being, for God's sake."

Slocum apologized and took special care to gently take Maud's hand to bring her up into the saddle in front of him. Despite her stiff posture, Slocum couldn't help but like the way her body fit tightly against his. This hellcat had been nothing but trouble, yet he couldn't help but admire her spunk.

As Slocum put his arm around her to steady her, Maud wriggled away from him.

"Just get this damn animal movin', so we can get this whole thing finished!"

"Yes, ma'am," Slocum replied, and spurred the horse into motion.

14

Slocum rode east out of Whoretown, with Maud seated sidesaddle in front of him, holding on with both hands to the saddlehorn. She had to hold on tight to keep from falling off. That was good. It kept her out of mischief.

Somewhere behind the houses an unseen dog barked. Like the rest of the local residents, it kept out of sight.

The moon was halfway to the zenith and shone big and bright. Slocum rode toward it, casting a long shadow behind him. Ahead, in the distance, was the runaway horse, a blur of motion on the prairie. Maybe the pursuers would be fooled into chasing it. Slocum hoped so.

North, about a hundred yards away on his left, across open fields, lay a belt of woods. Slocum drew abreast of the woods' end, passing it. Further east along the road there was a dip, a hollow. The curve of the slope stood between him and the houses, providing cover.

He swung the horse around to the left, plunging himself north. He hoped the ridgeline would cover his move, if anybody left behind was watching.

The horse was moving along at a nice clip, but not all out. Tearing along at full-tilt while carrying two riders would blow the horse out fast. Slocum wanted to conserve its reserves of strength as long as possible. He might have to draw on them to the fullest before this night was done.

There was the regular chuff-chuffing of the horse's rhythmic breathing, the muffled thud of hoofbeats against the turf, the rustle of tall weeds whipping against the animal's shanks, the creaking of saddle leather. An occasional stifled gasp escaped Maud when she was rocked by a rough bump.

The leading edge of the woods neared, a dark thin line of trees. Slocum glanced back, the ridgeline hiding all but the tops of the roofs of a few two-story houses.

He passed the trees on his left. The ridgeline suddenly played out, going from a mound, to a furrow, to a flat. Slocum was in a field, in the open in the moonlight, but the line of trees screened him from Whoretown.

In the open it was quiet, wind sighing through the trees, wailing across the distant plains. To the east lay miles of New Mexico prairie, and beyond that more of the same.

Slocum figured that if they put in enough distance between themselves and Bender, he and Maud could stop and rest. They shouldn't be too far now from where he had hitched the deacon's horse. Once they got to that point, things would get a little easier. As much as he liked having a warm body pressed up against his, the horse was starting to slow down from the weight. If they each had their own horse, the trip would go a lot faster, and they could go over to the tree line and set up camp. That way he could keep a keen eye out through the trees, and see if anybody came riding out after them from the direction of Whoretown.

Just as Slocum was thinking he had everything planned out nicely, he heard the faint mumbling of distant hoofbeats. Maud heard it too.

"What is that?" she whispered.

"I reckon you know as well as I do *what* it is. The real question is *who*."

He pulled his horse over to the trees, and then reined in, listening closely. The riders were definitely getting closer, and they were coming from the direction of town.

Quickly sizing up the situation, Slocum guided the horse slowly and quietly into the trees, until he figured they were well out of view from either side of the copse.

"Now try and keep your mouth shut for once," he said once he was satisfied with their cover.

"Why should I? Whoever's out there's gotta treat me better than you been," Maud said, a little too loud for Slocum's liking.

Just as he was about to hush her up again, he saw some movement out of the corner of his eye. On the plain leading from Whoretown he saw what appeared to be a posse. In the moonlight he could just make out Wessel and Hix. Obviously the bodies at Maud's place had been discovered.

"Hix!" Maud exclaimed to herself. But before she could call out to the marshal, Slocum cupped his hand to her mouth.

He brought his head down close to her ear and whispered: "I wouldn't do that if I was you. They just found two dead men at your house, Maud, and you were nowhere to be found. Nobody saw me come back into town, so the authorities are probably thinkin' that I got as far away as possible. That makes you their number-one murder suspect."

Maud wriggled a bit, but remained quiet.

" 'Sides that, who knows how honest your lawmen are? They could have their own stake in that sapphire, and are now thinking you might have known more than you were saying."

Maud started mumbling something at that. "Be careful

or they'll hear you," he cautioned, but removed his hand from her mouth.

Maud's first rush of fear was replaced by rising anger. Realizing how effectively she'd been boxed into a corner, she got so mad that she couldn't speak.

"That's the beauty of it, Maud. Now your fate is cast in with mine. You've got a stake in keeping me alive, if only because the people trying to kill me are going to be trying to kill you now too."

Maud glanced at the woods standing between her and Whoretown. She swallowed, finding her voice.

She said, "What're you talking so loud for? They'll hear us."

From beyond the trees came a few shouts. "They can't hear us," Slocum said.

"What're you doing, hanging around here for? Put some distance between us and the posse!"

"In due time."

Maud quieted her rising unease by mentally clawing out his eyeballs and roasting him on a spit over a slow fire. She wrinkled her nose. The woods smelled of musk, rot, and decaying vegetation. Most of the trees were evergreens, big shaggy bulwarks providing near-impenetrable cover.

After what seemed like hours, but was probably just minutes, the posse finally turned away from them and headed south. Maud breathed a sigh of relief.

"It ain't over yet," Slocum warned her, but brought their horse back into the clearing once he was satisfied that the posse was long gone. Spurring the tired animal faster, Slocum tried to make up for a little lost time. He knew they were getting very close now to the other horse.

When it looked as if their mount had had about enough, Slocum spotted the deacon's horse. They rode over to it and Slocum hopped off the lathered beast, helping Maud down after him.

His belly rumbled, reminding him that it had been a long time since he'd eaten anything, almost twenty-four hours.

Taking Maud by the arm, he walked her across the clearing, sitting her down on a large rock not far from the churchman's horse.

"Your friends are probably on the other side of the woods, if you feel lonely," he said.

"They're not my friends now, thanks to you."

"That's right, and don't forget it."

"I've got a long memory," she said meaningfully. "I never forget when somebody does me wrong."

"Good. Then maybe you can start remembering something that'll help me find the killer. Whoever stuck a knife in Dolores put a hurting on you too."

"Sure did, because they tangled me up with you, mister."

He went to the churchman's horse, speaking softly to it, easily. It sidled away from him at first, as far as its tether would allow. But he gentled it fast, and soon it allowed him to stroke its sides.

"That's the horse you stole from Deacon Mulch?" Maud asked.

"Uh-huh. Well, he can pray for me."

"He'll pray to see you hanging at the end of a rope."

The animal nuzzled Slocum, who said, "His horse likes me anyhow."

"Mister, that's the only friend you've got in this town."

"That makes us even. I'm not too crazy about Bender myself."

"Then leave."

"I've got some business to take care of first."

"Like you took care of Pierce's men?"

"Could be."

"Like you're going to take care of me?" Her voice was strong, steady.

"I've been taking care of you. Where'd you be if I hadn't done for those two on the porch?"

"That kind of help I don't need. I can handle ornery cowboys without killing them. I have all my life," she said, sounding tired.

"Maybe those two needed killing."

She looked up. "You could say that about most men."

"Especially me, huh?"

"You said it, not me."

"What do you suppose those two wanted, Maud?"

"What most men want, only they didn't feel like paying for it."

"They paid, but not in the coin they expected," he said. "Funny, though. Pierce sure seems minded to clean up Whoretown. He poured hellfire on the Doghouse."

"The saloon's been a thorn in his side for a long time, ever since he came to Bender. The Doghouse crowd's a bunch of drifters, rustlers, small-time outlaws . . . trouble-makers. But there was enough of them so Pierce couldn't bull them around, ride roughshod over them like he does to everybody else in town.

"Or at least there was until you came along," she added. "Thanks to you, Pierce had a reason to make a fight, and he had the law to help him get his killing done too."

"Soon as the thorn's out of his side, a couple of his guns come after you," Slocum said.

Maud's eyebrows knitted in a fierce frown. "What're you trying to say?"

"Just thinking out loud. Maybe Pierce decided to clean up you too."

"Why would he want to do that?!"

"I don't know. I'm a stranger here myself."

"For a stranger, you sure know a lot about what goes on in this town!"

"Not enough," Slocum said. "I don't know why Pierce wants to get rid of you."

"He doesn't!"

"Talk any louder and we can ask him in person."

"He doesn't," Maud repeated, low-voiced but intense. "Pierce doesn't come in my place, but some of his top men do. Engels, and Cal, and some of the others . . ."

"Engels, that's that big fellow who sides Pierce, right?"

"His bodyguard."

"And Cal, that's the one I stuck in the hand. What does he do?"

"He's a wrangler on Pierce's ranch."

"Cal was there the night that Dolores got killed."

"That oaf? He might be a good horse-breaker, but when he's out of the saddle, he can barely take two steps without tripping over his own feet. He's the last man to go sneaking around in the dark, doing murder.

"Besides, he was with Vangie all night," she said.

"He wouldn't need all night. All he'd need is a few minutes, just long enough to sneak upstairs ahead of me and hide in Dolores's room, waiting in the dark for us to show—"

"Mister, if you knew Cal, you'd know how ridiculous that is. He's not even one of Pierce's hired guns, he's just a wrangler. He's no sneaking cutthroat, jewel thief, and mastermind, which he'd have to be to do all that you claim the killer would have to do.

"Anyway, Cal was downstairs in the parlor when you went upstairs with Dolores."

"You sure?"

"Sure, I'm sure. You think I don't know what's going on in my own house on a Saturday night?"

"No, I guess you must, keeping track of business and all," Slocum said, thoughtful.

"You're damned right," Maud went on, oblivious to his change in mood. "They're all out to cheat me, whores and customers both!"

"You probably know where everybody is at any given time."

"Yes. No. I don't know." She was suspicious now. "What're you getting at?"

"I've got an idea," Slocum said.

Stony silence greeted his announcement. Maud folded her arms across her chest.

"You can get a girl by the hour or by the night, right?"

"Yes," Maud said tightly, giving away nothing.

"And you'd know which is which. Someone who pays by the hour had damned better be gone when the hour is up. I can't see giving away what ain't been paid for, not even time."

"Business is business. At least I give value for money. I'm not a thief," she said, sniffing.

"Now, when a girl goes upstairs with a man, she takes him to her room, and stays with him the whole time. And when he's done, she comes downstairs with him. You can't have the man wandering around upstairs, maybe sticking his head into another room to see what's going on. That's obvious enough."

"So? What's your point?"

"Just this. The crime wasn't discovered until morning, but that doesn't mean the killer had all night to do it. He struck when I went upstairs with Dolores, at eleven o'clock. Give him a minute or two to get into the room ahead of us, and another couple of minutes afterward to get things squared away. Not more than five minutes at the most.

"Now, who was upstairs at the time?"

"You," Maud said. "You and Dolores."

"Who else?"

"Pauline and her banker friend, Murray. They'd gone up to her room an hour before."

"That's it?"

"That's all that was upstairs at the time. This is a small town, mister. People get up with the sun and go to bed when it gets dark. Even on a Saturday night, eleven o'clock's late. Except for the overnights—and we don't get many of those—most of the customers have come and gone by eleven."

"You were downstairs, counting the house. There were a couple of girls in the parlor, as I recall."

"Berga and Sue. They were, uh, between engagements."

"Where was Chase?"

"Downstairs the whole time. I see where you're trying to go with this, but it won't wash. I *know* Chase was in the parlor when you went upstairs."

"How's that?" Slocum asked.

" 'Cause he was giving me hell for the liquor bills this month, saying I gotta start watering the whiskey. He and I were sitting pretty close to the stairs too, so we could both keep an eye on the comin's and goin's."

"You sure you couldn't have missed somebody? What if a girl snuck one of her favorites upstairs for free?"

"No way we wouldn't have caught them. Chase likes to keep close tabs on his investments," Maud said with a touch of bitterness.

"Okay, any more customers that night?"

"A couple of gents, by the name of Sim and Bailey, came right after you and Dolores went upstairs. They had a few drinks with Berga and Sue before going upstairs with them.''

"So how long before they went upstairs, you think?" Slocum asked.

"I don't know. About an hour I suppose," she said. "They stayed upstairs for an hour, then came back down and left right away. By that time Cal and Vangie had gone up. I let Sim and Bailey out, locked up again, put out the lights, and went to bed.''

"Sim and Bailey—that's the last two?"

"Yes. Two respectable townsmen who'd faint if you so much as up and said 'boo' to them. By your own logic, it couldn't have been them. They were downstairs while the murder was being committed, according to you.''

"Neither one could've gotten upstairs past you and Chase, huh?''

"Nobody could have.''

"What about Nedda?''

15

A storm was brewing. Out of the west, down from the mountains, came a flood of low dark clouds, streaming across the sky. Moonlit cloudy masses rushed east, churning, roiling, creating a sense of violent headlong motion. With them came great gusty winds, raw, damp, and cold. The smell of rain was in the air.

The stars were blotted out. The moon dimmed behind murky cloud veils, like a bright copper coin sinking into the depths of a river. Trees swayed, shaking their tops in the rising wind.

Slocum said, "Don't say I never gave you anything, Maud. Now you've got a horse too."

"A stolen horse," she said. "Stolen from Deacon Mulch too!"

" 'Tis better to give than to receive. I'm sure he'd agree."

"Not when it's his horse."

"Come to think of it, he didn't seem too overjoyed at that."

Not more than a few hours had passed since Slocum had gunned down Lonnie and Sutton. After they'd rested a good bit, he'd herded Maud, and the horses, back along

117

the trail by which he'd come, once again emerging north of the woods. He'd hefted Maud onto the back of the deacon's horse, while he climbed up on the saddled mount. Now, they both had horses. Their destination: Nedda's house.

Nedda lived alone, in a small house on the southern outskirts of town. Of course, Slocum couldn't just openly ride up to it, not with all the small bands of mounted men patrolling the area. He had to get there by the roundabout route.

He retraced the route he'd originally followed earlier that day, when first making his covert approach to Whoretown. He and Maud struck northwest, angling across the railroad line at a deserted spot north of Bender, in the outer darkness beyond the glow of the town lights.

Then they cut around, going west, then south, circling around behind the back of Bender's western environs. They rode in the lee of a ridge that ran parallel to the road south out of town. The ridge sheltered them from the worst of the chilly winds coming down from the mountains.

The dark was Slocum's ally, hiding him in its restless shadows. That was why he dared to ride on the lee of the ridge, rather than on the windward.

Progress was slow, thanks to Maud. She couldn't ride very fast, not when the only thing between her and her mount was a blanket spread across the horse's back.

"Next time, make sure you steal a saddle too," she said.

"I wouldn't have thought you'd have any trouble riding bareback, Maud."

"Ha-ha. When I ride, I get paid top dollar for it."

"I'm sure you're worth it."

"You can be sure, friend."

"You'll get paid." Slocum grabbed a fold of his shirt

at his side, rattling the jewel pouch nestled next to his skin.

"It's too much trouble for me to turn these baubles into cash, Maud. When our business is done, I'll turn them back over to you."

"Thanks a lot, considering that they're mine to start with. What about my money?"

"Let's not get ahead of ourselves," Slocum said.

Her not having a saddle was a help. It prevented her from trying to make a getaway. She couldn't ride fast without one, and if she made a break he could easily overhaul her. It kept him from having to watch her closely all the time. It slowed their rate of travel, but the need for stealth would have done that in any case. If they were chased, she wouldn't be able to make much of a run. He'd have to decide whether to throw her to the wolves or stay with her and make a fight of it.

For now, he needed her. She knew her way around town, and he didn't. He couldn't have found his way to Nedda's house without her. With her along, she was less likely to be sending him into a trap, not when the trap would be swinging shut on her too.

Once they were past the center of town, the houses were few and far between. What few there were stood sparsely scattered along both sides of the main road running south out of town. They were owned mostly by those who made their living in Bender and wanted a small piece of property of their own, or just wanted some elbow room where they didn't have to live with their neighbors right on top of them. Most of them did a little farming or ranching on the side. The bigger landholdings were farther away from town, sited along the watercourses and grazing lands.

Maud and Slocum passed a couple of dark houses. It was a rural community where folks went to bed early. Or maybe they didn't want to show lights for fear of attracting attention while a killer was somewhere out there, on the loose.

Or maybe the killer was somewhere in there, hunkered down inside one of those houses.

Maud was hunched forward on the horse, hands holding the reins and clutching the animal's mane to maintain her precarious perch. She was huddled deep in the folds of her cloak, which was wrapped tightly around her.

Little puffs of vapor from the horse's mouth faded into the cold night air. The wind swelled, sprinkling a patter of icy raindrops. Some fell under the back of Slocum's collar, trickling down his back, raising shivers. He turned his collar up, pulling it tight against his neck. A few fat drops splashed on his bare head.

His shirt cuffs were pulled down as far as possible over his hands for warmth. The cold was making his hands stiff and slow, when speed could be the margin of difference between life and death. He held the reins in one hand, sticking the other inside his clothes to warm it up. That seemed to help. He switched hands frequently, to keep both of them supple.

He asked, "How much farther?"

Maud pointed to a house about an eighth of a mile away, on the west side of the road. "There it is. But this is the craziest idea I ever heard of."

"We'll see," Slocum said.

He pointed his horse toward the house, Maud doing likewise. They angled across weedy fields, dry grass rustling under the horses' hooves. The ground, which had been soft and damp, was hardening up in the frosty air.

The house was a white box with a peaked roof. A light showed through the windows. Grouped near the house were a few outbuildings, a long gray shed and some

shacks. There was no one in sight. The house stood off
by itself, with no nearby neighbors.

Three riders came into view on the road, riding south
out of town. Riding hard.

Slocum and Maud were about halfway to the house.
Ahead and to the left was a stand of trees. Slocum pulled
up alongside Maud, taking hold of her horse's head harness. He didn't want the horse getting away from him now
with strangers approaching.

It wasn't much of a stand. The trees were more like
bushes, scraggly, with skinny trunks, the tallest not more
than ten feet high. Still, it was some kind of cover, along
with some tangled brush and a few big rocks.

The oncoming trio stayed the course, following the
road.

"Did they see us?" Maud said, her voice hushed.

"I don't think so," Slocum said. He reached inside the
saddlebag, hand resting on the shotgun stock, ready to
haul out the sawed-off and start blasting at the first sign
of trouble.

If the riders had seen them, they didn't show it, continuing unswervingly on their southbound course.

As the riders neared Nedda's house, the light went out.

The riders reined in at the blacked-out house, swinging
down from the saddle. They had drawn their guns. Two
ran up to the front of the house, and the third went around
to the back.

Maud was mystified. "Who are they? What do they
want with Nedda?"

"Maybe they had the same idea I did," Slocum said.

The house stood between Slocum and Maud and the
two men who had gone to the front, hiding them from
view. The third man darted around to the back, into the
yard between the house and the outbuildings. Gun in

hand, he darted up to the house, flattening his back against the wall beside the back door.

He was waiting for some signal. His dark form stood out against the white wall.

A breathless minute passed. The wind blew, pelting the trees with raindrops. Another minute passed.

Suddenly, from the front of the house, there was a scream, just as suddenly choked off. There was a flurry of shots.

The third man kicked open the back door and threw himself inside. As soon as he went through the doorway, he started shooting. Muzzle flashes flickered inside, like lightning.

He fired six shots, emptying his gun. Silence and darkness once more fell inside the house.

After a pause, the man materialized in the doorway, framed by it. He stepped outside. His hat was gone, and what looked like a handle was sticking out of his head at an odd angle.

He collapsed, spilling facedown into the yard. He lay still, motionless as a rock.

The back door hung open, the doorway a black oblong.

One of the riders' horses hadn't been securely hitched and broke free, running away. No one chased it. The two men who'd been at the front of the house were nowhere to be seen.

The house was dark, silent.

16

Slocum tied the horses up to the trees. He took the sawed-off shotgun from the saddlebag, closing it. The piece came together with a metallic locking sound.

"Let's go, Maud. I want to see what happened in the house."

"I'm not stopping you."

"You come too."

"No, thanks. If you want to risk your neck, that's your business. I'm in a different line of work."

"You were the one who was telling me how Nedda was a big dumb farm girl who wouldn't hurt a fly."

Maud eyed the unmoving body in the yard. "I'm not so sure now. She's one of those religious types, and you never can tell how that kind is going to jump."

"She's religious and she's working for you?"

"My money's as good as anybody else. You ought to know. You're stealing it. Besides, she's no whore. She's a drudge, a scullery maid. She cleans, fetches, washes, and does the donkey work around the house."

"Maybe she decided to go into business for herself."

"I always thought she was too stupid to steal."

"That's the kind you've got to watch."

Maud shook her head in disbelief. "I can't understand it. She was always spending her spare time with Deacon Mulch, doing charity work for the church."

"Yeah, well, she's not holding a prayer meeting now."

"If it's her inside the house. Maybe it's somebody else."

"Who? You told me that she lives alone."

"She does."

"If that's the way she treats company, I can see why she doesn't have more visitors."

"Who were those three men?"

"There's only one way to find out," Slocum said.

"Uh-uh. You go if you want to. Not me."

"I'm not leaving you here with the horses, Maud. Now, come on."

He took hold of her wrist and started forward, pulling her after him. She came along reluctantly, hanging back.

She said, "Why do we have to walk?"

"We can't sneak up on the house on horseback. Those three rode up bold as you please, and things don't seem to have worked out too well for them."

Freezing rain fell, sleeting slantwise. The tiny ice particles stung where they struck bare flesh. They made pattering noises against the ground, like sifting sands. It would help cover the sound of the duo's approach.

The wind was at the backs of Slocum and Maud, beating against them, the icy cold creeping through their garments like water soaking through a sieve. They walked bent forward, crouched almost double.

The house stayed dark, silent.

Slocum held the sawed-off in his right hand, and Maud's sleeve in his left. He approached by a route that put the outbuildings between them and the house, screening them from view.

Maud said, soft-voiced, "Give me a gun so I can defend myself."

"Who's gonna defend me against you?" said Slocum.

Ice pellets fell hissing on dead weeds and grass, forming a slippery crust which crunched underfoot. The outlines of the outbuildings and house were blurred in the murk.

They reached the back of the barn, leaning against it. Their hair and eyebrows and garments were powdered with wet ice crystals. The narrow roof overhang did nothing to protect them from the sleet.

From inside the barn came the sound of a heavy body lurching against stall rails and clomping hoofbeats: a horse. Only one, from the sound. The animal was restless but not panicked. The barn door was closed, so it had missed the brunt of the mayhem.

Slocum's hands were stiff with cold. He flexed his fingers, working them. He beat his hands against his thighs to restore circulation. After a bit, the life came back into them. They lost their numbness and started to hurt, but at least the flexibility had returned.

Slocum peeked around the corner of the barn, at the house. The back door hung open on its hinges, each gust of wind slamming it against the wall with a loud bang. The sound reminded Slocum of the trapdoor falling open on the gallows, dropping the condemned into eternity at the end of a rope. It was a reminder he could have done without.

The open doorway looked like a black coffin standing upright. At the threshold sprawled the dead man. He lay facing away from the house, with his arms stretched out in front of him.

There was a handle sticking out of his head, an ax handle. The blade was buried deep in the top of his skull.

From it gushed a large dark puddle of gore, which was being churned by the sleet.

Ice crystals covered his back, making him look like he'd been covered with glazed vanilla frosting.

The heft and balance of the sawed-off in his hand was a comfort to Slocum.

From the road, fresh hoofbeats sounded, slowing as they neared the house. Maud frowned.

"More gentlemen callers," Slocum said.

17

Marshal Hix and Deputy Dick Wessel slowed their horses when they saw the two horses hitched to a fence post in front of Nedda's house. They reined in, stepping down into the rutted road, which was frozen solid and smeared with a thin coating of slushy snow. The icy rain was tapering off, replaced by a fall of fat wet snowflakes. The flakes made soft plopping sounds as they pelted Wessel's hat, which was pulled down tight on his head to keep the wind from blowing it off.

They had their guns drawn, and hitched the horses to the rail and stood over to the side, at the northeast corner of the white picket fence enclosing the front yard. On the other side of the fence was a line of man-high bushes, bare now, but still providing some cover from the snowy winds.

The house was a simple structure, basically a one-story white-painted clapboard box with a peaked roof. It fronted the road. The front gate hung open.

"I don't like the looks of this," Wessel said. "The horses must belong to the three men we saw ride out of town like bats out of hell, but where are they?"

"They must be around here someplace," Hix said,

snowflakes clinging to his walrus mustache. When he spoke, the flakes looked like they were going to fall off, but they never did. Flecks of tobacco clung to his yellowed teeth.

"They can't have gone far. We took out after them right after we saw them swing wide of the road guards. They were only a couple of minutes ahead of us," Hix said.

Wessel was only half listening. He was up close to the strangers' horses, eyeing them closely.

Hix said, "What're you doing over there?"

"These look like Pierce horses," said Wessel.

"How can you tell that? Hell, one horse looks pretty much like another."

"I can tell. I've got an eye for horseflesh. These are big fine animals, the kind that all of Pierce's guns ride. The regular ranch hands ride ordinary cow ponies, but the shooters ride these big mounts."

"They could be stolen. That'd explain why those fellows were riding so hard and fast. Steal something from Pierce, and you better ride fast."

"Why'd they stop here, at Nedda's of all places?"

"When we find 'em, we'll ask 'em," Hix said. "In the meantime, let's stop mooning about the horses and start dealing out some professional-style law enforcement, like the folks of this county pay us to do."

His breath melted the snowflakes on his mustache, but more fell to take their place.

"It was a mistake to deputize Pierce's bunch," Wessel said. "They're more trouble than they're worth."

"They're a tough bunch," Hix said.

"They'll tear up the town unless they get whipped into line."

"They're rowdy but they mean well. They're high-spirited young fellas."

"Maybe some of those young fellas got a hankering for a woman and decided to drop in on Nedda."

Hix looked at him. "I said they're high-spirited, Deputy, not blind. That's enough palavering. Let's see what kind of a situation we got here."

They moved along the fence, past the line of bushes, and into the unbuffered wind and snow, which hit them in the face. Hix clapped a hand on top of his hat to keep it from blowing away, mashing the crown.

There was about a quarter inch of snow on the ground. It crunched under their boots as they stepped. They had to swing wide out into the road to get past the horses. When they moved in front of the house, the wind lessened.

There were tracks in the snow, footprints leading through the open gate and across the lawn. The lawmen went through the gate. Two sets of footprints led up to the front of the house, while a third went around to the back.

It had begun to snow so hard in the last few minutes that the footprints were already beginning to fade under the newly fallen snow.

Wessel, who was in the lead, indicated the footprints going around to the back of the house, then gestured that he was going to follow them. Hix nodded, motioning that he would tackle the house from the front.

Wessel angled off to the side, where he could see the side wall of the house and some of the backyard and outbuildings. The snow on the ground brightened the scene, but the wind-driven snow whipped into his face, cutting down visibility, so the two factors, the brightness and the wind, tended to cancel each other out.

Wessel swung wide as he moved to the back of the house so no one could surprise him by lurking behind a blind corner. He didn't know what he would find, but he had his gun ready. The snow tended to muffle sound, but one thing he could hear was the wailing wind.

Hix advanced at the front, gun leveled. Behind curtained windows, the house was dark. The front door was firmly, solidly shut.

A ball sat on the top step of the front stairs, teetering near the edge. It was about the size and shape of a child's ball, and that was funny, because Nedda lived alone and didn't have any kids and wasn't the type to let the neighbors' kids play on her property.

Hix started climbing the steps. That set the ball into motion, making it rock gently back and forth. It was not so much round as melon-shaped, and lay on its side.

Something about it unnerved Hix, who was a hard man to get a rise out of. Maybe it was because a melon doesn't have hair. He stepped back onto the walk at the foot of the stairs.

The melon rolled off the top stair and fell the rest of the way, bouncing down the steps. It was heavy and made thunking sounds each time it hit a riser. It plopped into the snow at Hix's feet, looking up at him.

It was a head.

A man's head. The expression on its face wasn't nice. Hix thought he might have recognized its owner, but he couldn't be sure because the grimace of fear, pain, and outrage on it distorted the features into something inhuman.

The head had part of a neck too. The cut was very clean.

Hix looked up. The front door was still solidly shut, the house still dark inside. Was it his imagination, or was one of the curtains slightly moving, as if someone had lifted the edge to peek outside?

With his gun raised, the hammer thumbed back, Hix started backing away from the house. The head took a little half roll toward him, and for one awful instant Hix had the feeling that the damned thing was following him.

But the head came to a stop against a bump in the ground, and Hix realized that its seeming volition was just an illusion. That didn't mean that whoever had separated the head from its body was an illusion, though.

He backed away, trying to look everywhere at once. He took small, careful, almost dainty steps that looked comical in a man of his size and ruggedness.

This is going to take some serious strategizing, he said to himself.

Meanwhile, Wessel had found the body in the backyard. He stood near the corner of the house, with his back to the wall.

He didn't like that open back door. He didn't like it at all. There were footprints leading into the house, and a much shorter set of prints leading out of the house, where the man with the ax parting his hair had taken a few staggering steps before flopping facedown on the ground.

But there was no second set of prints, left by the escaping killer while making a getaway. Which indicated that the killer was still inside the house.

He didn't like the banging door either. Each time it slammed into the wall, it sounded like the crack of doom. The unholy racket made it hard to hear anything else.

A shadow of motion flickered on his right side, away from the door, where his attention was focused. He sensed more than saw a heavy bearlike form looming beside him. His heart skipped a beat. Then he saw that it was Hix, and his heart started beating normally again.

Then Hix stuck a gun in his back.

"It's no joke. I'll blow a hole in your liver," Hix said, his tone conversational but fraying at the edges. He smiled tightly, showing yellow teeth.

Wessel didn't think it was a joke. He knew it was real,

horribly, frighteningly real. It crystallized a lot of suspicions he'd been nursing about Hix for a long time, and he realized that he'd guessed right, only Hix had thought faster and this was the payoff.

Hix took the gun out of Wessel's hand. He eased down the hammer, then tossed the gun aside. The pressure of his gun muzzle boring into Wessel's back was a reminder that death was near.

"Another one, eh?" Hix said. "Who is it? Engels?"

He prodded Wessel with the gun. "I don't know," Wessel said.

"It looks like him. A big man. Engels is a big man too," Hix said. "He don't look so big now. Who'da thunk Nedda had it in her?"

"What's Nedda got to do with it?"

"What? You mean you ain't figured it out yet, a bright fella like you? I'm disappointed in you, Deputy. It's a cinch you'll never make marshal."

"Nedda, the murdered whore, Lonnie and Sutton, Pierce—and you, Hix—you're all tied up together."

"Well, sure, it's easy for you to put it together now that the bodies are piling up and I've got you under the gun. But you still ain't got the half of it, and from the look of things, you never will."

"Suppose you tell me, Marshal."

"Stalling, eh? I'd like to oblige you, but it's cold out here, and Nedda's waiting inside. It ain't polite to keep a lady waiting. Not that Nedda's no lady. She's a damned fury, is what she is. The Big Boss sent three men to do her in, and instead she did for them, all three of them. With an ax. It don't hardly seem natural that a female could be that ornery, does it?"

"The Big Boss? Who's that? Pierce?"

"You ain't even close." Hix's toothy grin widened, while his eyes were narrow. "Pierce takes his orders from the Big Boss, same as I do, same as plenty of others in this town do, only most of them honkers ain't got the faintest idea who's sitting at the top of the heap, pulling the strings on the rest of them.

"Call yourself a manhunter, Deputy? Sheeyit, you couldn't find a turd in a sugar bowl. Here you been a peace officer in Bender for the last couple of years, rattling doors, rousting drunks, and generally walking around with your head up your ass, and all the time the sweetest little outlaw setup of all time has been going on right under your nose and you never got a whiff of it, you dumb son of a bitch."

"I'm not as dumb as you think, Hix. I knew there was plenty of things about this town that didn't add up: all the stagecoach robberies with no survivors, the travelers who disappear into the mountain passes and never come out, the bones found bleaching out in the desert, Pierce and his gang of guns, when that phony ranch of his that doesn't do enough business to meet a weekly payroll. Sure, I knew there was something plenty rotten in Bender, but like everybody else, I held my nose and kept my eyes shut."

"Well, now you're going to shut them permanently," Hix said. "There's a crazy woman in this house and she's got to be stopped pronto before she can do any more damage, and you're elected. You're going in through that door and I'm coming in right behind you, and when the smoke clears, I'll be the only one standing.

"We've jawed enough. Start walking."

"And if I don't?" Wessel said.

"Then I'll kill you where you stand, set fire to the house, and burn the bitch out," Hix said.

"Like you did at the Doghouse? I knew there was something wrong about the way that went down, but I couldn't put my finger on it."

"Those small-timers get big ideas. Sneaking around, night-riding, doing their petty rustling and horse-thieving, they see things they shouldn't. They got too big for their britches, so it was time to light a fire under 'em.

"Come to think of it, why should I stick my neck out trying to take Nedda in her own den? Hell, the last fellow who tried that lost his head over her, heh-heh. Reckon I'll just play it safe and put the house to the torch. When she tries to make a break, it'll be a turkey shoot. A good hot fire'll warm up those tired old bones of mine too.

"Course, that leaves you holding the short straw, Deputy."

"Going to shoot me in the back, Hix?"

Hix took a few steps back from Wessel, away from the house. He said, "I'm going to give you a sporting chance, Deputy. Go for your gun."

Wessel glanced at his gun, lying on the ground ten feet away. "Some chance," he said.

"Call it a professional courtesy to a fellow lawman."

"There's only one lawman here, Hix, and that's me. You're a murdering crook."

"In another second, there won't even be one. Make your play."

Wessel gathered himself for the attempt, hoping against hope that he could live long enough with Hix's bullets tearing through him to reach his gun and put a slug in the marshal.

"Make your play, Deputy, or by God, I'll kill you where you stand!"

Wessel tensed his muscles, readying himself for the annihilating blast.

It came like a thunderclap, only it wasn't Wessel who was struck by lightning.

Hix's head erupted like a quarter stick of dynamite going off in a watermelon, vaporizing into a red cloud that hung in the air for a few beats after the body hit the ground.

Slocum stepped into view from behind the corner of the barn, holding the smoking sawed-off shotgun.

"Never mind about that, Marshal," he said.

18

Out in front of the house, a horse neighed, and there was a sudden clatter of hoofbeats. Slocum moved past the corner of the house, into the open.

A horse raced north along the snow-covered road, a dark form running alongside it, clinging to the saddle. With a spring and a kick, the figure vaulted up onto the animal's back. It leaned far forward, hugging the horse's neck, presenting as small a target as possible.

It was Nedda, her long unbound hair flying behind her like a comet's tail.

She was too far away for the shotgun, so he switched the sawed-off to his left hand and used his right to snake out the six-gun stuffed in the top of his pants.

He pointed the gun at her just as she flashed behind the screen of bushes, obscuring his aim. He fired one shot at her, unable to tell if he'd scored or not.

She kept on going, and then she was out of range and there was no point in wasting another shot. Snowflakes swirled around Slocum, whirling like a dust devil. The wind shifted and the white column collapsed, spilling out snow.

Nedda rode north, not slackening, a dark blur arrowing

between the frosty ground and snowy air. In the murky zone where earth met sky and neither could be told apart, the wild-haired rider vanished.

Slocum lowered his gun, turning. Hix lay sprawled on the ground. Wessel stood nearby, motionless, not having moved since Hix was gunned. Huddled against the barn, holding on to the corner of it and peering around it, was Maud.

Slocum stuck the gun in his belt. He held the sawed-off shotgun with seeming casualness, pointing it at the ground, but it would take no more than an upward flick of the wrist to bring the blaster in line with Wessel.

He squatted, hunkering down to pick up Wessel's gun from where Hix had tossed it. Jarred from his immobility, Wessel started forward, only to check himself an instant later, when he saw Slocum shake his head. Wessel stalled, and it was as if he'd never moved at all.

Slocum smiled with his lips, not unpleasantly. He rose, brushing the snow off Wessel's gun. He popped out the cylinder, letting the bullets spill to the ground.

The gun emptied, he pitched it underhand to Wessel, who came alive long enough to catch it. He put it in his holster.

"You can reload later, maybe, when we understand each other better," Slocum said.

"I'm starting to catch on," Wessel said, glancing at Hix. "What I don't get is your part in all this, Slocum."

"You will. For now, just keep remembering that I saved your hide.

"But don't get cocky about it," he added.

He motioned to Maud, beckoning her. "Come on in and join the party."

She pushed off from the barn, crossing the yard. She made a wide detour while drawing abreast of the body of the axed man. She neared Wessel and Slocum, suddenly drawing to a halt when Hix's corpse swam up in her field of vision.

"Now you've gone and done it, mister. I never thought I'd see anybody bring Hix down," she said, awed despite herself.

"I don't think the law's going to kick about it," Slocum said. "Ain't that right, Deputy? Or should I say, 'Marshal'?"

"The former marshal being deceased means that the next man in line moves into his spot, and that's you, Wessel. Congratulations on your promotion, and don't forget who gave you a leg up."

Wessel rubbed his hands. An uncharitable observer might have thought that he was gloating, but he might well have been merely trying to warm his hands.

"I've got no quarrel with you about Hix," Wessel said, looking guardedly at the other. "But I've got plenty of questions I want answered, Slocum."

"You'll get answers, but you might not like them."

Again Wessel eyed Hix, this time shrugging. "I like them so far."

Maud looked around. "What happened here? Who killed those men—*Nedda*? Who were they and what did they want? Why did Hix want to kill his own deputy?"

Slocum said, "Who's the man with the split head?"

"I'm not sure, but it looks like Engels," Wessel said.

"Let's be sure." Slocum crossed to the body, the others following. They looked down it, Maud grimacing, Wessel saying, "Whew!"

Wessel crouched, reaching for the ax handle with both hands. Slocum gestured with the sawed-off, motioning him away.

"I was just going to lift it so I could see the face," said Wessel.

"Not that I don't trust you, Marshal, but I'd feel better

if you didn't put your hands to an ax. I'll do it," Slocum said.

He gripped the ax handle with his left hand. The blade was in so deep in the dead man's skull, it wasn't coming out easily. Slocum lifted the handle, raising the head up on its neck, pulling the face out of the ground, revealing it. Even masked with snow and mud, it was recognized right off by Wessel and Maud.

"Engels," Wessel said, Maud nodding.

Slocum let go of the ax handle, and the head flopped back facedown on the ground.

"Who's Engels?" Slocum asked.

"Pierce's foreman," said Wessel.

Slocum nodded, remembering him from the storming of the Doghouse. "Big mean-faced hombre," he said.

Wessel shrugged. Slocum said, "Pierce had an important job for him, but he messed up. He didn't reckon on Nedda."

"I guess none of us did," Wessel said.

"She always worked her butt off, never shirking, never complaining," Maud said. "I should've known it was too good to be true."

Slocum gestured toward the house. "Let's go in."

"Is that wise? Nedda might be going to get help," Wessel said, glancing north, where the road remained empty.

"I don't think so," Slocum said. "The thieves have had a falling-out. Pierce sent Engels and the others to take care of Nedda, get rid of her. Only she got rid of them."

He turned to Wessel. "How'd you and Hix happen to show up?"

"There's road guards on the way out of town. We were on patrol, and happened by the post just in time to see the three men trying to slip past. Come to think of it, Hix wasn't too keen on tailing them. He said that he didn't want to leave the town short-handed. But it wouldn't have looked good for him not to go after them, so away we went. When he saw what had happened, he decided it was a good time to get rid of me,'' Wessel said.

"That's good," Slocum said. "It means the gang is getting scared. Some of them can see the writing on the wall, and they're getting ready to burn up the territory.''

"Good for who? Not for the town.''

"It may be the only chance Bender has," Slocum said. "Anyhow, Nedda can't go to the others, now that they've tried to kill her. That buys us some time, I think. A little time.''

"Maybe the road guards'll stop her," Wessel said.

"Too bad for them," Slocum said. "Let's go inside.''

Maud said, "Yes, let's! Before I freeze to death!''

Slocum gestured with the sawed-off, indicating that Wessel should go first. Wessel crossed to the house. Maud started after, but Slocum motioned for her to halt.

"Best not get between me and the marshal yet," he said.

They went to the doorway, first Wessel, then Slocum, with Maud following. Beyond the threshold lay mostly darkness and silence.

Wessel said, "One of them may still be alive.''

"I doubt it," Slocum said. "That Nedda strikes me as a pretty thorough worker.''

Wessel stepped through the doorway. When he was a few paces inside, Slocum said, "Wait up." Wessel stood still. Slocum stepped into the doorway, striking a match on the inside wall.

With a spit and a hiss, the match flared into brightness, its expanding globe of yellow light revealing a kitchen.

There was a table with a red-and-white checked tablecloth and some chairs. There was a cooking hearth, now cold, dark. There was a sink and cabinets and a waist-high counter. The curtains on the windows were made of the same red-and-white checked fabric as the tablecloth.

Blood was tracked and smeared across the floor. Opposite the back door, in the far left corner of the room, an archway opened into another room, of which only a part could be seen. In that part, on the floor, were bodies and more blood.

Then the match flame nipped Slocum's fingers and he snuffed it out, bringing the return of darkness. The light had revealed a lantern sitting on the countertop.

Slocum struck another match, not looking directly at the light to minimize his loss of night vision. He crossed to the counter, the slippery floor causing him to watch his footing.

It was a railroad lantern, about half the size of a milk can, with a bucket-type handle.

"Looks like Nedda was getting ready to make a getaway," Slocum said.

A third match lit the lantern. The lamplight was yellow-gold with big platinum-white arcs and curving bands that were reflections of the lens.

Maud stepped inside, standing with her back to one side of the open doorway. She stood very straight with her hands behind her back. Snow blew through the door, winds ruffling the curtains.

Thin watery light from the lantern spilled into the next room. Wessel stuck his head inside. On the floor, near his feet, he saw a gun in the hand of an arm that lay outstretched on the floor. No body, just an arm. The body lay farther away, on the other side of the room, mingling what remained of its mangled limbs with those of a second, headless corpse.

Wessel stuck his head back out. "It's a charnel house."

"It's warm, though," Slocum said. "Close the door, Maud."

"Leave it open. It stinks in here," Wessel said, gagging, one hand at his throat.

Maud looked at Slocum. Slocum shrugged. Maud left the door the way it was, open. She moved along the wall, a few steps away from the door.

Outside, the wind blew the door against the wall, again and again, banging, flapping.

19

Slocum said, "A couple of months ago, a young woman from a wealthy family in St. Louis—the name doesn't matter—came out here to meet her fiancé. He's a mining engineer at a settlement further west of here, over the mountains. She never arrived. Neither did the stagecoach she was on. It had vanished without a trace somewhere en route through the mountain passes.

"Not long ago, some prospectors came across what was left of the coach, at the bottom of a steep mountain road with a sheer drop-off. It was supposed to look like an accident, like the coach had gone off the cliff. Animals got to the bodies, so by the time they were found, they weren't much more than bones. Still, one of the skulls had what looked like a bullet hole in it, and there were some funny things about some of the other skeletons, like they'd been shot.

"And all of their valuables were missing. Scavengers wouldn't carry those off, except human scavengers. Of course, they could have been stolen by the prospectors themselves when they found the wreck. Or somebody could have come along before them, found the wreck, looted it, and moved on without ever telling anybody what they'd found.

"The family did some digging. It didn't take them long to find out what everybody in these parts has long known: that the mountain passes are bad medicine, and that it's safer to go around them than through them, because a lot of those who start through them never come out the other end.

"It's long been suspected that a gang haunts the passes, preying on travelers, robbing and killing them and burying the remains. The only reason the prospectors found the stagecoach was because a rock slide had uncovered it. Nobody's ever tried to see if the story about the gang is true. Or if anyone did, the gang must have got them somehow.

"The mining engineer had heard of me. Through a third party he got in touch with me. The official verdict on what happened to his fiancée, and the rest of the passengers and the driver, was death by accident. He didn't buy it. He hired me to look around and see what I could find.

"I found out that three bad hombres had been seen at the last way station where the stagecoach had stopped before going into the pass. The three were Brett Lloyd, Gordo Mapes, and—Trav Bannock."

Slocum paused. Wessel stroked his chin, saying, "Bannock, the man you killed. It's starting to add up."

"Don't go toting up the sum yet. You haven't heard it all," Slocum said.

He went on. "Lloyd, Mapes, and Bannock were thieves and killers, but they'd managed to keep ahead of the hangman. They were seen at the station on the same day that the stagecoach stopped there. Not at the same time, but on the same day. They were seen and recognized by the stationmaster and some other witnesses, who were mighty glad to see them go. Later, when the stagecoach was first missing, the three of them were remembered and their names came up. But with no sign of the missing coach, there was no case, nothing to charge them with. No crime, technically. It's listed on the books as 'death by misadventure.' "

Wessel said, "But not with you."

"Not now. At first, I wasn't sure. I knew the three of them in passing, and there wasn't much I'd put past them. Bannock would cut your throat for two bits, if he thought he could get away with it. Brett Lloyd was supposed to be a more decent sort—he wouldn't kill you unless you got in his way, or unless he was fairly well paid. And Gordo would shoot you down just for the fun of it. The fact that they were in the area when the stagecoach disappeared weighed heavy in the scales against them.

"I started looking for them, thinking it might be a good idea if we all had a little palaver. That was about a month ago. Since last summer they had split up and gone their separate ways, though they were all still in the territory. Turned out I wasn't the only one looking for them.

"They got Gordo Mapes first. He was bushwhacked, by person or persons unknown. Shot off his horse by a rifle. No shortage of suspects, since so many people hated his guts. The law was content to mark the books closed on him, without bothering to look for his killer. They figured whoever'd done it had done them a favor. Funny thing, though. There was a legal bounty on Gordo's head, for a killing he'd committed since breaking up with the others. Whoever killed him could have picked up a nice couple of hundred dollars reward, but nobody ever claimed the money.

"Next came Brett Lloyd. He was coming out of a gambling hall in Desert City at night, and when he walked past an alley, somebody shot him in the back and killed him. No suspects, no clues.

"I had missed Gordo by a week, Brett Lloyd by a few

days. I was close behind Bannock, only a few hours too late. As it was, he was still alive when I found him, barely. He'd been dry gulched outside town and taken to a side canyon where his captor could work on him with fire and a red-hot knife. Bannock was all staked out, and they were out in the middle of nowhere, where nobody could hear him when he was tortured.

"The one who was working on Bannock didn't hear me when I came up behind, maybe because of all the screams. He was a skinny galoot with a scar running down one side of his mouth, giving him a hangdog look. I don't know who he was, and I didn't get a chance to ask him."

"I do," Wessel said. "That sounds like Dutton, Nucky's brother. With that scar on his mouth, it'd have to be him. He's been missing for the last few days."

"You can find him at the bottom of a pile of rocks in the canyon," Slocum said. "When I found him, all he had in his hand was the hot knife he used on Bannock. I had a gun.

"It was too late to do anything about Bannock. I cut him loose and tried to make him as comfortable as I could, covered him up with a blanket. He talked readily enough. He wanted revenge, and he knew me, and he knew the best way to get revenge was to tell me what I needed to know.

"He and the others *had* been planning to rob the stagecoach. That's why they were in the area, to scout it out. They didn't care who saw them because they planned to beat it out of the territory after the holdup and never come back. After stopping at the way station for water and stores, they rode on ahead, up the mountains into the pass. They went to the spot where they'd already planned to launch their ambush, took cover, and waited for nightfall and the arrival of the coach.

"As the time neared, they discovered that somebody

else had the same idea. They weren't alone in that lonely stretch of the pass. There was another gang there, of about twelve riders. Bannock and the others didn't like those odds. They stayed hid and hoped that the newcomers wouldn't stumble across them.

"Then it was time and a team of horses topped the rise, hauling the stagecoach into view. The mystery men struck, riding it down. They massacred the driver, shotgun messenger, and passengers, shooting them down out of hand. They were after the strongbox which the stagecoach was hauling that trip, carrying a big cash shipment. They had a good spy system. Bannock and friends hadn't even known the cash box was aboard. They had merely planned to rob the passengers. They were fit to be tied when they saw the mystery men making away with a small fortune in gold right under their noses!

"But there wasn't anything the three could do about it. Like I said, they didn't like the odds for a fight. And the way every living soul on the stagecoach had been wiped out took some of the starch out of Bannock and company.

"The gang wore masks, hiding their faces. A band that big and that deadly should've been known to one of the three outlaws, but they'd never heard of them and had no idea who they were. If they'd known of them, they wouldn't have come within fifty miles of the pass. The way that the gang worked showed they were sure hands at this business, and had done it many times before.

"After making sure that all the victims were dead, the main body of the gang rode off with the cash box, riding east, back out of the pass. They left behind three men to get rid of the evidence. The trio loaded all the bodies in the coach. Two of them got up on the coach and drove away, with their horses tied behind. The third rode along-side. They went west, deeper into the pass.

"By now, Bannock and his friends were starting to get

over their fear, and were working up a pretty good mad about the payday which, as they saw it, had been snatched away from them. That the rest of the gang was gone and showed no signs of returning didn't hurt either. Bannock and the others rode out of where they'd been hiding, after the stagecoach. They were careful to keep pretty far back, out of sight, and they kept their eyes and ears open just in case the rest of the gang should decide to come back.

"The stagecoach halted at a lonely stretch of mountain road, where there was about a thousand-foot drop-off. The outlaws ran it off the cliff, horses and all. Then they rolled some big rocks over the side, starting a landslide which buried the wreckage. Searchers later went up and down that road many times, passing that spot without seeing what was buried far below at the bottom of the cliff. It wasn't until months later that rainfall caused a rock slide which uncovered it, allowing the prospectors to find it.

"Their job done, the three masked men mounted up and started east, back the way they came. They hadn't gone very far when they rode into the guns of Bannock and his boys, laying in wait for them. They were shot dead.

"Earlier, the masked men had made a painstaking search of the victims, going through their bags and clothes, picking them clean of their valuables. The cash box had been the gang's target, but those who stayed behind to clean up made sure they did just that. Their scavengings made up a tidy sum for Bannock, Lloyd, and Gordo, who took them off their dead bodies.

"One of them had a jeweled brooch, which he'd taken off the girl from St. Louis, the mining engineer's fiancée. It had a blue stone, a sapphire, an old family heirloom. Bannock came across it while searching his man's body. He pocketed it without telling either of the others. They were busy doing their own plundering. They left the bodies in the road, where they had fallen.

"They were a lot closer to the eastern side of the pass than the west, close enough to reach the flat and hole up before first light. They hadn't robbed the stage, there were no witnesses, so they didn't have to light out of the territory after all. And there was that cash box too. Maybe they could get a lead on that loot and cut some of it out for their own. So, that's what they did—go east, back out of the pass, and go to cover.

"Now, I'm guessing at what happened next, but it makes sense in light of the facts. When the stagecoach failed to arrive at its next stop on the far side of the hills, search parties went out, but they found no trace of the men killed by Bannock and his boys. When they'd failed to rendezvous with the rest of the gang, the others must have gone back out looking for them. It must've given them quite a start, knowing that what they thought was a perfect crime was known to someone else, someone who might start dogging them.

"In any case, they got rid of the bodies, so the searchers never found them.

"Bannock and friends drifted around, working the nearby towns to get a line on the gang. They were all three booze hounds, and Bannock and Gordo were loud-mouths, especially when they'd had a skinful, which was most of the time. So it wasn't too long before one of them said something out of turn, and it got back to the wrong people. Suddenly, somebody was dogging *them*.

"Bannock had a lick of sense more than his two friends, so one day without warning he up and left them. They didn't know where he was or why he'd gone. Now, neither of them trusted the other, and when it was obvious that Bannock wasn't coming back, they split up.

"It could be that Bannock was setting up his ex-partners, because it wasn't long after that that Gordo Mapes killed. Then it was Brett Lloyd's turn. The mountain gang was getting its own back.

"Bannock was a lot of things, but he wasn't yellow, not where greed was concerned. He was still trying to get a line on that stolen cash box. He'd learned enough to know to look here, in Bender. He didn't know that he'd walked into the snake pit.

"He rode into town on Wednesday. On Thursday night, he was at the House of Seven Sisters, boozing and whoring it up. Am I right, Maud?"

Maud shrugged. "I don't talk about my gentlemen callers, but under the circumstances, I'll make an exception. Especially since he's dead?"

"He's dead," Slocum said. "That night he was at your place, he was lushing it up, bragging his big brags, and playing the big man. I didn't have to be there to know, because I knew him, and I knew that's how he behaved around women. He gave that blue stone to Dolores, to impress her."

"She wasn't that impressed," Maud said. "She thought it was a fake. We all did. A sapphire that big . . . it couldn't be real."

"That's what Bannock thought, or you couldn't have pried it away from him with anything short of dynamite. Funny, he was risking his life to get a lead on that cash box, when all the time he was walking around with a valuable star sapphire in his pocket."

"Hysterical," Maud said dryly.

"The next day, Friday, Bannock was caught out of town. I don't know what he was doing there. Maybe he was lured away, or maybe he was doing some snooping when he was taken. Either way, he was taken by—what'd you say his name was, Deptford?"

"Dutton," said Wessel.

"Dutton," Slocum repeated. "Here's where there was a change in the pattern. Gordo and Lloyd died fast. Bannock was taken alive and tortured. Dutton wanted to know where the blue stone was.

"I don't know how the gang had learned of the brooch, but I can guess. Nedda told them. She was one of them all along, planted in Maud's house as a spy."

"Nedda a spy? You're crazy," Maud scoffed.

"Look around here and tell me who's the crazy one," Slocum said. "Having a spy in your house makes perfect sense. Only men of means are allowed inside those doors. Bankers, ranchers, miners, drummers . . . They do plenty of talking, especially when they've had a few and they're trying to impress the ladies. You can overhear lots of things that'd be useful to the gang, like when payroll shipments are being made, or valuable cargo is being freighted across the pass, or when a promoter is traveling through with a wad of cash, traveling alone. I wonder how many left your house to set out on their way and were never seen again."

"Too bad you weren't one of them," she said.

"It wasn't for lack of trying on Nedda's part, but that comes later. She was perfectly placed. Who'd pay attention to her? Yet she was always there, in the background, changing sheets or carrying away glasses, her chores as drudge giving her free run of the house at all times.

"When she saw Bannock flash that blue stone, she knew what it meant. The girl from St. Louis's family had put out a circular describing her and her belongings at the time she'd turned up missing, including a description of the jewelry. That circular went out to all law enforcement agencies in the territory. Hix would've gotten one. The gang put out the word to keep a lookout for the missing jewel. If it should turn up, they'd know that whoever had it had taken it from their murdered compadres in the pass.

"And then the blue stone turned up, right in the gang's hometown. Nedda got word about it to her secret masters. The next day, Dutton got Bannock. Bannock was tortured to find out what he knew about the gang, and who else he'd told. He hadn't told anyone, but Dutton didn't believe that, and kept on working on him.

"Then I came along, and Dutton went out. I learned what I've told you from Bannock. I'd already learned some of it, and guessed some more, but that helped fill in a lot of the blanks. Not long after finishing his story, Bannock died.

"Bannock's chest and—well, you know—had been worked on pretty thoroughly with a hot knife, but his face was mostly untouched. That gave me an idea. I couldn't bring Bannock in the way he was, not without raising questions I wasn't ready to answer. I dragged him over to the fire and laid him across it. The burning hid what had been done to him. His head was untouched. I buried Dutton in a shallow grave and covered it over with rocks, so the coyotes wouldn't dig him up too soon. I wrapped Bannock in a blanket and tied him across the back of his horse. I covered up the fire pit and the other signs that somebody had been at the site. I rode out, with Bannock and Dutton's horse in tow. When I was far enough away, I let Dutton's horse go.

"That was Saturday. I'd stayed the night at the site, to get things squared away. I rode into town, to the marshal's office, to claim the reward on Bannock. I claimed that he'd gone for his gun, only I'd shot first, and that he had fallen across the fire and gotten burned. Nobody doubted my story, not openly. There was a price on Bannock's head, he was wanted dead or alive. The only ones who'd reason to doubt me were the gang members.

"As we now know, Hix was one of them, but he never

let on while I put in my claim for the reward. I couldn't be sure of him, or you, Wessel.

"I knew that the blue stone had been given to Dolores. Bannock had told me before he died. I went to Maud's house that night, and sure enough, Dolores was wearing the sapphire. I played it cagey, watching to see who else might be dogging the jewel, or me. I made like I was one of the boys, drinking and laughing it up."

"You played your role too well. You got stinking drunk," Maud said.

"I may have been a mite over-enthusiastic, but I wasn't as drunk as I looked."

"Sure."

"By then, the wheels were already turning. Nedda had her orders. I paid no attention to her. In a roomful of beautiful women, who watches the scullery maid? My mistake. Nedda already had her orders, and was waiting for the chance to act on them.

"That chance came when I got ready to go upstairs with Dolores."

Maud, skeptical, said, "What were you going to do, question her?"

"I figured it wouldn't hurt to mix a little business with pleasure," Slocum said. "Again, my mistake.

"Nedda went upstairs ahead of me. I didn't see her go, because I wasn't looking for her, and I'll bet nobody else saw her go either. If they did, they wouldn't think twice about it, figuring she was just carrying out some routine chore.

"She hid inside the darkened room, waiting. Dolores and I came along. She went into the room first, to light the lamp on the bureau. Nedda stabbed her with the knife, killing her instantly. Dolores died without a sound, or if she made one I didn't hear it. I stumbled into the room. Nedda clubbed me with something, laying me out. I don't know what she hit me with, but I've got a big lump on the back of my head and it hurts.''

Maud said, ''One of the brass candlesticks wasn't in its usual place in the parlor today. I didn't think much of it at the time, but . . .''

''A candlestick. Is that all? It felt like a tomahawk.''

''I think I'll have it gilded.''

''Nedda lit the lamp on the bureau. She lifted Dolores onto the bed and laid her out, tearing off the necklace. That's what left the mark on Dolores's throat. She made sure to take off my gun belt and hang it on the chair, out of reach, for later. She hauled me across the room and wrestled me into the bed, beside Dolores. She's a big husky farm girl and could do it. You've gotten a good look at her handiwork tonight.

''She tilted the mirror on top of the bureau with the lamp behind it so it would reflect plenty of light on the scene, so she could take a last long look and make sure that everything was just so. When it was all to her liking, she turned out the lamp, peeked into the hall to make sure that the coast was clear, and went outside, closing the door behind her. Then she went back downstairs, as little noticed as she had been when she went up, and went back to her chores.

''She knew that I'd paid to stay the night, so Dolores's room would be undisturbed until daybreak. If I'd managed to come around before then, I'm sure she had some plan set to finish me off. When I still hadn't come around by first light, she decided to set the ball rolling herself. It was easy. She just opened up the room and started howling.

''The rest you know,'' Slocum said.

20

Wessel said, "Why'd Pierce and Nedda have a falling-out?"

Slocum shrugged. "My getting away must've spooked Pierce. He didn't know how much I knew. As long as there was a chance I might get away, he and all the gang were in danger. Being of a suspicious turn of mind, and naturally suspecting everybody else of being as crooked as him, he might've thought that my getting away was no accident, that Nedda might have crossed him and warned me as part of some plot of her own.

"Then, when two of his men turned up shotgunned to death on Maud's front porch, Pierce must've really got worried. He didn't know who did it: me, Maud, Nedda, or somebody else who was moving against him. And now that I think on it, it's my guess that Pierce sent those two to get rid of you, Maud, like he sent the others after Nedda."

"Why me? I'm no threat to him," Maud said.

"Pierce didn't know that. He couldn't be sure that you weren't in it with Nedda, or if Nedda had said something accidentally or even on purpose that would've let you know what was really going on. Or even if you'd seen something, some clue, that would have helped you add it all up and come out with the right answer.

"Or maybe he's just the kind that believes that dead men—and women—tell no tales."

"Then Pierce is the head of the gang?"

"Why not? He and his riders lead a double life. He's a rancher and they're his hands. It's all legal and on the up-and-up and nobody suspects a thing. Only, I did some checking, and found out that the few livestock that Pierce sends to market wouldn't pay the county tax on his spread for a month. No, the gang poses as cowboys, until they get word of a gold shipment or some other likely prospects going out through the pass. Then they show their true colors as night-riders, do their robbing and killing, make the evidence disappear, and get back to the ranch before first light. The ranch is the perfect hideout. It doesn't even look like a hideout," Slocum said.

Wessel said, "That's about how it looks to me, except I'm not so sure that Pierce is the head of the gang, not the way Hix was talking right there at the last. He bragged up somebody he called the Big Boss. Not Pierce, he said. It was somebody else, somebody that nobody would ever guess."

"Did he say who it was?"

"No, but it wasn't just idle talk. He had no reason for shucking me, since he was going to kill me."

"Hmmm, maybe I shot him too soon."

"Not by me, you didn't!"

"We can leave the problem of who's the gang leader for later. Our main woe is Pierce and his riders," Slocum said. "They've been hurt tonight, but they've still got the guns and the numbers."

"What do you suggest?" said Wessel.

"Me, I'd rather kill than run," Slocum said. "I'm tired of freezing my butt off in the out-of-doors. Besides, the gang's hurting and there'll never be a better time to hit them.''

''After Hix, I'm not sure who I can trust,'' Wessel said.

''Hix was trying to kill you, so I figure I can trust you. And I could've killed you and didn't, so you can trust me.''

''The two of us, against Pierce's crowd?''

''Three,'' said Maud. The others looked at her.

''It's not like I have a choice,'' she said. ''If they catch up with me, I'm dead. I'd rather get them first. I can shoot. Ask him,'' she said, indicating Slocum. He nodded.

Wessel was doubtful. ''Three against the whole gang. It's still bad odds.''

''Maybe we can even them up somehow,'' Slocum said.

''How?''

Maud said, ''What about the other deputies?''

''They're the very men I can't trust,'' Wessel said. ''Nucky's the brother of Dutton, the man you killed, Slocum. And Stringfellow's a great friend of Hix.''

''What about the townsfolk?''

''Again, how would you know who to trust? Some of the citizens might be secretly in league with the gang, and betray us at the worst possible moment.''

Slocum said, ''I know where we can get a whole passel of ornery, up-on-their-hind-legs-and-fighting citizens, with every one of them guaranteed to hate Pierce's guts and give no quarter.''

Wessel said, ''Who?''

''You've got a jailhouse full of them.''

Wessel thought about it for a moment, then chuckled. ''You know, it just might work.''

''It better,'' Slocum said. ''Okay, Marshal, just to show I trust you, you can load your gun now.''

''Thanks.'' Wessel took bullets from their holders on

his holster, feeding them into chambered cylinders of his revolver.

"I hope you've got plenty of ammunition, because you're gonna need it," Slocum said.

Maud said, "What about me?"

"Marshal," Slocum said, "I'm sure you wouldn't mind stepping outside like a gentleman for a minute so Maud and I could have a private word."

Wessel held his now-loaded gun thoughtfully, weighing the heft of it, not pointing it at anything. "I'm *not* so sure."

He glanced at Maud. She said, "Go ahead, Marshal. I'm not afraid of him."

"No, I guess you're not," Wessel said.

"Or any man," she added.

"Tell that to Pierce," Slocum said.

"I will. With lead, same as I'd do to any man who'd try to steal from me," she said.

Wessel shuffled his feet, uncomfortable. He thought it was some kind of lovers' quarrel. "I'll go round up the horses."

"Be right with you," Slocum said.

Wessel went outside. Maud held out her hand palm up. Slocum reached inside his shirt, pulled out the pouch of jewelry, and gave it to her.

She made it disappear into one of her hidden pockets. "Don't think I won't inventory it piece by piece later." She held her hand out again. "Now, my money."

"Later."

Her face stiffened, her eyes flashed. "What're you try-ing to pull, you dirty bastard?!"

"Wessel I can trust, at least for now. You, I think I can trust, but I'm not entirely sure. I'll just hold on to that money for safekeeping, as a kind of insurance policy.

Later, when the dust settles, I'll give it all back to you, every cent. You have my word on it.''

''What's the word of a thief and killer worth?''

''It's as good as a whore's, I reckon.''

''Don't be so sure!''

''Me holding on to the money is my way of making sure you don't try to go into business for yourself and cut a little private deal with Pierce or anybody else. Plus, this way you've got a stake in keeping me alive. Those are the kind of odds I like,'' Slocum said. ''Of course, you could make a complaint to the new marshal, if you think your money'd be any safer in his hands.''

''Why? So he could steal it? Not a chance!''

Slocum tilted his head toward the doorway. ''He's calling us. Let's go.''

He followed Maud outside, into the snow, the wet, and the cold. Slocum glanced past the yard, to the stand of trees, which could be glimpsed through gaps in the snowfall.

''We'll have to bring in the horses so they don't freeze,'' he said.

''That's nice for the horses. Too bad you don't show some compassion for human beings,'' she said.

''I like horses. Tell you what I'm gonna do, Maud. I'm going to give you something that's even better than money. A gun.''

He reached into his hip pocket, pulling out the ivory-handled silver pistol he'd taken from her earlier.

''To hell with that popgun. I want a real man-stopper,'' she said. She went to Hix's corpse, which looked like a snow-covered sugarloaf mountain with hands. She picked up Hix's gun and wiped it clean of snow with her scarf.

''The marshal's gun should do it,'' she said.

''Careful where you point that thing, Maud. Remember,

I'm going to be killing the men who're trying to kill you.''

She thought about it, lowering the gun to her side. The sawed-off being held not so negligently by Slocum might have had something to do with her forbearance.

''You're a smart businesswoman, Maud.''

''If you get shot, whatever you do, don't bleed on my money.''

''Yes, ma'am.''

21

The guard post on the south road was unmanned, seemingly deserted. It was a hundred yards or so outside of town. A lantern hung on a fence post on the east side of the road. It threw an oversized oval of yellow light slantways across the road. Nearby, a horse was tethered to another post. It was the guard's horse. The guard lay facedown in a ditch by the roadside, on the same side as the horse and lantern.

Lamplight fell across the ditch and the man. Outside the yellow oval, it was dark. A house was set back from the road. It too was dark. North, up the road, lights showed in the town, cold and distant. Between the post and the town there was darkness shot through with snow, and open empty fields.

Slocum and Wessel toed the ditch, looking down at the dead man. Maud stayed on her horse, unwilling to dismount. "I've seen dead men before," she said. "More than my share on this night, though."

The dead man's head was twisted at an unnatural angle, looking backward over his back. The purple-white face was bruised, eyes staring.

"Nedda was here," Slocum said. "No ax, so she broke his neck with her bare hands."

"It's Lex, Nucky's asshole buddy," Wessel said. "The two of them were manning this post. Nucky's got to be around here somewhere, probably in a ditch."

But Nucky was nowhere in the immediate vicinity. "If she killed him, she hid him good," Slocum said.

"Maybe she didn't kill him. Maybe she carried him away," Wessel said.

"What for?"

"How should I know what goes on in the mind of a madwoman? Maybe she wants to fricassee him."

"Well, we've got bigger fish to fry. We can't afford to spend any more time around here. I'm sorry about your man, but what's done is done."

"I'm not. Sorry, that is. Lex was one of the men I had my doubts about. Nucky too."

They mounted up, and they and Maud rode into town. The streets were empty, most of the buildings dark. It was so quiet that snowflakes could be heard hitting the walls and windows.

East along a cross street, a couple of blocks away, what could have been a lone figure on foot flitted into view. The wind blew a whirl of snow, and when it cleared, the figure was gone.

Lights showed in the jailhouse window. The jail had been built back in the old Spanish mission days, and was as much fort as jail. It was a one-story square stone cube with small barred windows, occupying the southeast corner of the town square.

Inside, the vaultlike space had been divided into two areas. In the front was the marshal's office and administrative area, and in the back were the cells. The building fronted the south side of the square. Just inside the door, there was a small open area, its far end marked off by a waist-high wooden railing. In the center of the rail was a hinged gate. The rail stretched from wall to wall. On the right side of the gate, inside, was the marshal's desk. Behind the desk, on the wall, was a relief map of the county. On the other side of the space, against the opposite wall, stood a locked gun cabinet. Above it, the wall was papered with wanted posters and circulars.

Near the marshal's desk, there was a wood-burning iron stove. In it, a fire was crackling, radiating heat in the immediate area. In that area was a card table. Around it sat Stringfellow, Nucky, and Cal. They were smoking, drinking, and playing cards.

Beyond, in the back, were the cells. Four in all, two on each side of the center aisles. One cell held the Doghouse boys, Jeeter, Pete, and two or three others. Beatings had been handed out, and they had the marks to show for them. Pete's face showed he'd gotten the worst of it. It was a mass of swollen discolorations, with one eye almost swollen shut. They were all hungry, thirsty, cold, and dirty.

In the cell across from them were the women, Myrtle Mullins and Viola. They hadn't been beaten, except for Myrtle, who had a mouse over one eye from when Nucky had backhanded her for mouthing off.

In the cell next to the Doghouse boys was another group of men who'd been arrested separately, a couple of drunks and a pair of petty thieves who'd tried to take advantage of the chaos by taking what wasn't theirs and had gotten caught. The drunks hadn't been handled too badly, but the thieves had been beaten as badly as, if not worse than, the Doghouse boys.

There was a pounding on the street door. Stringfellow, Cal, and Nucky looked at it. "Go see who that is," Stringfellow said, returning his gaze to the cards in his hand.

Nucky and Cal looked at each other. Cal held up his

hand, the one that wasn't holding cards. The center of it was thickly wrapped in gauze bandages.

"I'm wounded," Cal said.

"Hell," Nucky said. He put down his cards, carefully laying them facedown on the table so the others couldn't get a glimpse of them. He pushed back his chair, crossing to the rail. He paused with his hand on the swing gate, looking back at the others, saying, "And no peeking!"

He opened the rail gate and went to the door. It was a heavy slab of ironbound oak with a sliding lookout panel at eye level. He opened it and looked out.

"It's Wessel," he said.

On the other side of the grate, Wessel said, "Open up, Nucky, you damned fool!"

Stringfellow was vulturelike, with sly avid blue-gray eyes. He said solemnly, "Better open it."

Nucky closed the lookout panel, and unbolted and unlocked the door. While he was doing it, his back was to the table. Stringfellow lifted Nucky's cards, stealing a quick peek. Cal was carefully blank-faced.

Nucky whirled around, but Stringfellow was sitting calmly back in his seat, studying his cards. Cal remained blank-faced. Nucky glared.

Wessel pushed the door open, bulling in, letting in a blast of cold air that swept the length of the building. Snow dripped off him. He held a leveled gun.

Behind him came Slocum, stepping to the side so he'd have a clear line of fire with the sawed-off shotgun he held raised. When they saw him, Stringfellow and Cal pushed back their chairs and started to rise, Stringfellow clawing for his holstered gun. Then they saw the sawed-off shotgun and froze.

Stringfellow eased his hand off his gun butt. He winced in pain, remembering his wound, clapping his hand to his thigh where the bandage was. His leg folded under him and he sat down.

Nucky was the last to get the play. He had turned and was starting back toward the table, Wessel behind him. He didn't even see Slocum come in. Wessel pulled Nucky's gun from the holster. Too late, Nucky clapped a hand on the empty holster. Wessel gave him a boot in the tail that sent him sprawling to the rail.

"Next stop, Boot Hill," Slocum said. "Any takers? No?"

Cal placed his hands down on the table. Stringfellow let go of his wounded leg and did the same. Nucky lay stretched on the floor, upper body leaning on the rail. He held up his hands, shaking his head.

Maud stuck her head inside the jailhouse door. "Still quiet out here."

"Keep watching," Wessel said.

"I know what to do," she said, ducking back outside.

Wessel prodded Nucky with his boot toe in the rump until the latter managed to open the swing door and crawl through it. Wessel went around the table, taking String-fellow's gun. Cal didn't have a gun.

Stringfellow gaped, his mouth hanging so far open that his cigar butt fell out of it, into his lap, with a shower of sparks. He flinched, beating away the red-hot embers—

Suddenly there was a gun at his head, the muzzle press-ing his forehead. He froze, staring up at it. The gun was in Wessel's hand, and Stringfellow had heard the hammer being cocked as the piece was put to his head.

"Watch those sudden moves, String. You almost got yourself hurt," Wessel said easily.

Stringfellow nodded, barely moving his head. Wessel took the gun away from his flesh.

Stringfellow managed to find his voice. "Yuh—yuh loco?"

"Shut up and get over there, with your other two friends. Move!"

Stringfellow limped over to one side, where Cal and Nucky had already been herded. From where he stood, Slocum could have dropped the three of them with one blast, and they knew it.

Wessel got the cell keys down from the wall. Slocum kept the others covered. With his free hand, he lifted Cal's cards, eyeing them.

Cal said, "Hey!"

"That's the second bad hand you got today, Cal," Slocum said.

"Huh?"

He and Wessel hustled the trio back into the cell area. The prisoners were quite intrigued by this latest development, even the drunks.

"What's this?" Jeeter said, disbelieving.

"There's a new program," Slocum said. "The ins are out and the outs are in. The jailers are the prisoners and the prisoners are the jailers."

Pete cackled. He got it.

"Listen up, you Doghouse boys—and you ladies too," Slocum said. "You're dead, all of you. Pierce's gang is going to kill all of you, *unless you kill all of them first*."

Pete spoke first, without hesitation. "Glad to! Just let me out of here, son, and I'll let 'er rip!"

He cocked his head, staring intently with his good eye at Slocum. "Say . . . don't I know you?"

"You were shooting at me this morning."

"Was that you? Sorry, son. What the hell, I missed. No harm done. Glad I didn't hit you. Looks like you turned out to be all right after all."

Pete beckoned confidentially, lowering his voice. Behind a hand, he pointed a thumb at Wessel, saying, "What about him? Are you sure you can trust him?"

"He's okay," Slocum said.

Pete straightened, leering cockeyed at Wessel. "So you finally saw the light, eh, Deputy? Bletchley and me was doing some night herding one time—strictly unbranded mavericks, you understand—when we saw the whole gang without their masks, splitting the loot from some holdup. They knew they'd been seen, but they didn't know by who. They figured it was somebody from our crowd over to the Doghouse, though. It was only a matter of time before they tried to kill us all."

He pointed a stabbing finger at Stringfellow. "He's one of 'em! Tweed was too. I knew they were just waiting for an excuse to gun me down legal, and today they had it. So, I opened up on 'em! Didn't do too badly neither! I killed Tweed and turned Stringfellow into a gimp, haw-haw-haw!"

"You hateful old drunk, I'll—" Stringfellow began.

"You ain't gonna do nothing, so shut up," Slocum said.

Wessel said tiredly, "If you knew all this, Pete, why didn't you and Bletchley tell somebody? Tell me?"

"I wasn't sure about you," Pete said. "You might be okay, but the gang's everywhere. Stringfellow's one of them, and Nucky's one of their spies."

"You lying son of a bitch!" Nucky said, then recovered. "I mean, what gang?"

"The one you're going to take a ride on the gallows with," Wessel said. "What about Cal? Is he one of them?"

"Not him, he's too dumb! He's so dumb, he probably doesn't even know there is a gang," Pete said.

"Thanks, I think," said Cal.

Wessel stuck the long key into the massive lock and turned it, tumblers clicking over with a sound like muffled clockwork.

He opened the door, motioning to the Doghouse boys in the cell. "Out."

They exited, replaced by Stringfellow, Nucky, and Cal. "Why me?" said Cal. "Pete said I was okay."

"Maybe yes, maybe no," Wessel said. "But you work for Pierce, so it's better to keep you locked up for now."

He closed the cell door, shutting the three in. Before he could turn the key, Pete said, "You don't have to lock 'em up so fast. We've got business to settle with those boys, only this time there won't be two of them holding one of us, while the other puts the boots to him, like there was last time, eh, boys?"

The Doghouse boys agreed. Wessel said, "That's for dessert. Pierce first."

Pete considered it, head bobbing with quick birdlike motions.

"A fair bargain," he said, speaking for the group. "Killing Pierce will be a real pleasure."

Wessel once more reached for the key. Stringfellow said heavily, "When Hix finds out about this—"

"He's retired," Wessel said.

"Dead," said Slocum.

"I'm marshal now." Wessel turned the key, locking the cell. Stringfellow slunk to the rear, sitting on the edge of a bunk.

Wessel released Myrtle and Viola from their cell. The group started toward the front. Some of the petty crooks and the drunks cried to be let out.

Wessel looked at Slocum. Slocum said, "Why take chances? Keep them behind bars and sort them out later. The Doghouse crew we know we can trust. They have to fight, if only to save their own necks. Otherwise, Pierce'll hunt them down like dogs."

"We get the idea, sonny," Pete said. "Don't worry,

we ain't none of us gonna run. We got a lot of evening up to do with Mr. High-and-Mighty Pierce!''

Wessel unlocked the gun cabinet. In it were fine weapons, rifles and guns, Winchesters and Colts, and boxes and bands of ammunition. They were eagerly received by the Doghouse crew.

Wessel held up what looked like a bundle of smooth sticks. ''Look what I found. This should come in handy.''

Dynamite.

They gave Myrtle a shotgun and told her to guard the prisoners. Slocum said, ''A lot depends on surprise, so we can't have the prisoners talking out of turn, trying to warn Pierce. Course, once the cat's out of the bag, one more shotgun blast won't matter. If Pierce is tipped by one of you prisoners, none of you will live to see what happens next.

''And that goes for you damned drunks and the rest of you, savvy? If one of you looks like he's gonna yell, all you others better shut him up first, else that shotgun'll speak.''

''I get you,'' Myrtle said, looking through the bars at Stringfellow. He squirmed, backing into a corner.

She said softly, but not fondly, ''Remember when you gave me the back of your hand? Remember when I said I was going to get even?''

''You can't leave her back here with that shotgun! You can't!'' Stringfellow said.

''Shhh,'' said Slocum. ''Hush, now.''

He said to Myrtle, ''You know, the idea here is to not jump the gun.''

''I know,'' she said. ''Everything in its own sweet time.''

''If you shoot in advance and warn Pierce, I'll shoot you.''

She made shooing gestures. "Away with you. We'll be fine here. Won't we, String?"

He was silent. Slocum went away, getting ready for the showdown.

22

A good cigar, thought Slocum, puffing away. It was one of Hix's, from a box he kept in his desk. It was the one bit of warmth and comfort allowed to Slocum on this cold lonely night vigil, and even it had a purpose.

He was not worried about the smell of the cigar smoke giving him away, betraying the presence of a lurker. Not up here, on top of the jailhouse roof, near the front of the building, where Slocum now lay.

At the front of the building, the facade rose three feet above the top of the flat roof, forming a waist-high wall. Slocum sheltered below it, crouching beside it, out of sight. A folded blanket lay beside him, on which were laid some weapons and a few bundles of sticks.

It had turned colder and the snow was now sticking, layering the empty streets with white. Enough time had passed since the shooters had taken their position in the empty store diagonally across from the jail for the snow to have covered up the tracks of their footprints. That was good. Slocum had worried about it until the snow had blotted them out.

In the store were Pete and a couple of his boys. From time to time, Slocum could hear the click of one of their gun barrels rapping against the store window. If he could hear it, so could Pierce. It hadn't happened for the last ten minutes, allowing Slocum to hope that they had settled into a silent wait.

The empty store and the jailhouse formed a kind of inverted L in the southeast corner of the square, a potentially deadly trap with Pete's group in the store, Wessel and Maud and the others armed and waiting in the jail, and Slocum up on the roof, smoking a cigar, waiting.

He'd rigged things so he was the only one waiting outside in the snowstorm. Some planning! On the other hand, he wouldn't have trusted anyone else in his spot.

The cigar was burning down, more than half gone. Slocum wondered if it was time to light another. He couldn't be without a cigar when the critical time came, fumbling around with matches during the showdown.

He was about to reach into his pocket to fire up another of Hix's fine cigars when he heard the riders coming.

At first, he wasn't sure he'd heard it. Then the wind blew, and he couldn't hear anything. Then the wind fell, and he could hear the sound of riders approaching again, and when the wind blew again, hard, he could still hear them coming.

He peeked over the top of the facade wall. A dozen riders entered the square from the north end. The snow muffled the sound of the horses, like cloths wrapped around their hooves. But they were so close now that there was no way not to hear them.

They rode up in front of the jail, reining in. Slocum ducked his head back, out of sight, but not before seeing that the riders were masked, bandannas and scarves hiding the lower halves of their faces.

They were right below him, and he could spit on them. Instead, he touched the cigar's lit end to the fuse that was sticking out of the top of some bundled sticks of dynamite.

The fuse caught, sputtering, then sizzling like a Fourth of July sparkler.

Below, a mask-muffled voice said, "Now we'll finish off those Doghouse scum for good, men!"

"And the other prisoners? We finish off them too, Pierce?"

There was a shot, a bullet hitting flesh, a horse rearing up, a body falling to the ground.

"Idiot! Calling my name!" said the first voice that had spoken. The other would speak no more.

"Tell our friends inside to open up," Pierce said.

Slocum stuck his head over the top of the parapet, holding the lit bundle of dynamite. Even though he was masked, there was no mistaking Pierce, the sheer animal bulk of the man seated on a mount the size of a quarter horse. He was almost right below Slocum.

Slocum said, "Heads up, Pierce!"

Pierce's head whipped around, trying to see who had spoken.

The gun he held in his hand was still smoking.

"Up here!"

A few of those on the far edge of the group got it first, since their angle of vision took in more of the top of the jail. Some started pointing and shouting, and a few guns began to swing up.

Following the direction they were pointing, Pierce looked up in time to see Slocum drop a bundle of dynamite in his lap.

Slocum ducked back, behind the parapet.

The blast shook the building, knocking some bricks loose. Heat, fire, noise, and smoke filled the street.

Pierce sailed into view, rising above the top of the parapet. The blast had lofted him skyward—half of him anyway, the upper half, from the waist up. The lower half was somewhere down there in the chaos, shredded to atoms.

There was a crash of breaking glass as windows were knocked out, followed by crashing volleys of a cross fire from the shooters in jail and those in the store.

Pierce dropped out of sight. Slocum lit another bundle of dynamite, shouting, "Heads up!"

The shooting stopped, as the defenders reacted to the signal by taking cover. Some shots crackled as the outlaws began to return fire.

Slocum tossed the dynamite in their midst, unleashing another blast. The effect was terrible, wonderful.

His only regret was what it did to the horses.

More cross fire, than a pause as the third and final bundle of sticks was thrown. After that, all that remained was to pick off the last holdouts who still had enough life left in them to shoot a gun.

In less than sixty seconds, they were gone too.

"A turkey shoot," said Slocum.

Then the silence was broken by a shout from Stringfellow: "No! Don't!" drowned out by a shotgun blast.

As Myrtle later explained, "He yelled."

Church bells started to ring.

23

"What's going on with those damned church bells? Why don't they stop ringing?" Wessel glanced toward the church, frowning. "They've been clanging and clanging for a long damned time."

"Maybe we better go see," Slocum said.

They started toward the square, leaving behind the jail-house and the smoking remains of the gang.

Maud raced after the others, falling in beside Slocum. "I'm not letting you out of my sight," she said.

"What's Chase going to say about that?" Wessel said.

"It's not what you think," Maud said, sniffing. "My interest in Slocum is purely business."

"Shucks, I'll bet you say that to all the fellows," Slocum said. "Whatever did happen to Chase?"

"Who cares? Useless bastard," Maud said.

"The last time I saw him was this afternoon, when he was lighting out of town in search of you, Slocum," Wessel said. "I haven't seen him since."

"I hope he finds me soon. I want to get my gun back."

"You'll get it a bullet at a time," Maud said.

They all had to speak loudly, to be heard over the bells. Abruptly, the tolling stopped, its last steely note shivering away in the swirling snow.

A small crowd had gathered in front of the church. They stood looking up at the steeple. They were joined by Wessel, Maud, and Slocum.

In the belfry were two struggling figures, battling desperately.

Slocum said, "That's Nedda, but who's she fighting with up there?"

"Why, I believe that's Deacon Mulch," said Wessel.

Now Slocum recognized Deacon Mulch, the preacher whose horse he'd stolen. The deacon clambered up on the sill of one of the pointed belfrey arches, trying to get away. Nedda lunged. The deacon slipped, falling.

The crowd recoiled as the deacon fell screaming, crunching to earth at their feet.

Wessel winced. There were some groans, and one of the spectators, a man, screamed.

Somebody else pointed, shouting, "Now what's that crazy woman doing?"

Nedda tied a noose in one end of the bell rope, pulled it tight around her neck, and stepped off into the steeple shaft. She fell about halfway to the floor before she reached the end of the rope. Her neck snapped, breaking the thread which held her to life, catapulting her deathward.

She hung bobbing from the bell rope, ringing the bell.

Slocum and Wessel approached the deacon. "Pore little fellow," somebody said behind them.

Wessel and Slocum leaned forward, peering. Wessel said, "What's that in his hand? Looks like he's holding something."

"A gold chain," Slocum said, for the ends of a broken gold chain were protruding from the deacon's clenched fist.

He stepped on the dead man's wrist, prying open pudgy fingers that had clenched something in a death grip. It was a sapphire brooch.

Slocum pocketed the blue stone. "That tears it. Now we know who's the Big Boss, the leader of the gang."

"The little deacon?" said Wessel, astonished.

"None other."

The bell kept ringing. Maud was waiting, with her hand out.

"Time to pay the piper," Slocum said. He lowered his voice confidentially. "Say, Marshal, there won't be any trouble in putting through that reward on Bannock?"

"Well, now, that could be a problem, since you didn't kill him."

"That'll be our little secret. Otherwise, that bounty's going to go to waste."

"I'll see what I can do."

"Thanks, you're a real friend."

"Provided I get half."

"What! You're a crook! Okay, half," Slocum said.

"Done," said Wessel.

"You're both crooks," Maud said. "And I want a third."

24

"Sometimes, Maud, a man's got a certain hunger, a burning need inside that he's just got to fill, no matter what, come hell or high water," Slocum said. "I'm sure a woman of the world like you understands such things, Maud."

"Sure, I understand. Indulge yourself," she said. "Eat hearty, because you're going to need all your strength for later, when I get you upstairs."

They were in the kitchen in the back of Maud's house, where they'd gone after the celebration in town broke up. They were alone in the house, just the two of them. Slocum sat at a table, facing the back door. He was feeding the inner man with a meal of cold chicken, bread, cheese, and wine, with apple pie and coffee waiting on the sideboard.

Slocum was ravenous, wolfing it down. Between mouthfuls, he said, "You cook good, Maud."

She laughed. "I don't cook. Nedda was the cook around here."

He paused, eyebrows lifting. "Hope it's not poisoned."

"It's not. I had some for lunch."

"I was dying of hunger anyhow." He went back to his meal.

Maud finished counting her money, for the second time. "Lucky for you it's all here."

"I told you, I'm a man of my word!" he protested.

"Uh-huh. Well, it's all here anyway."

Slocum cleaned his plate. Outside, the night waned, the grayness beyond the curtained windows lightening. "How about seconds?"

She came over, standing beside him at the table. "I hope your other appetites are just as keen."

"Oh, they're keen, all right." He pulled her down on his lap, nestling the soft rounded warmth of her bottom against his thighs and groin.

She put her hands at the back of his neck. He embraced her, giving her a long kiss before coming up for air.

"Ummm," she said.

"That's the sweetest thing I've tasted yet," Slocum said. "Course, I haven't tried the apple pie yet."

A shadow fell across the curtained back door window and the door was suddenly kicked open from the outside.

Standing framed in the doorway was Chase, holding Slocum's gun, pointing it at Slocum seated across from him at the table. The middle part of his face was taped and bandaged where his nose had been broken. A triangular guard built up around his squashed nose to protect it made him look like a white-beaked snowbird.

"No pie for you," he said, his voice distorted and made comical by the face wrappings. He could afford to sound comical. He had the gun, the drop.

Slocum eased Maud off his lap, saying, "It's me he wants."

Chase shook his head. "I want it all. The money, the blue stone, the jewels, all! I've been sitting outside with my ear to the keyhole, listening. Laughing. Just like I'll be laughing in another minute, when you'll both be dead and it'll be all mine."

Maud stood up straight, her eyes and voice level. "You'd kill me, Chase?"

"I'm tired of you," Chase said, watching her face closely for the reaction, disappointed when there wasn't any.

The overhang of the tablecloth where it fell off the edge of the table hid Slocum's hands from Chase's view, and Chase was mostly watching Maud, so he didn't see Slocum reach into his hip pocket for the instant it took him to fish out Maud's ivory-handled little silver pistol and bring it up past the table, and when he did see it, he was still an instant too late.

Slocum shot the eyes out through the back of Chase's head. Chase fell backward.

Slocum got up, went to the body, and relieved it of its holster and gun.

"Thanks for returning my gun. I'd have hated to lose it," he said to the body.

"Take him out the back door and dump him with the rest of the garbage," Maud said.

Slocum looked at her.

"I was tired of him anyway," she explained. "Hurry up and let's go to bed."

"I still ain't had that apple pie yet," he said.